Sugar Snapped

A JULI BUTLER MYSTERY
BOOK TWO

BARBARA WITEK

OLIVERHEBERBOOKS

*Thank you to my family, friends, and readers
who encouraged me to continue this series.
And to Oliver Heber Books for believing in me and giving me
the platform to make it a reality.*

One

I walked out my front door into the quiet of the summer morning and smiled, remembering my childhood. I was happy to be back home, which is something I never thought imaginable not too long ago. New Hope, Connecticut came alive in the summer, I especially loved the fireworks. The warm breeze tickling my face and the golden rays of sunshine warming my skin were both calming and invigorating.

Ever since the first murder New Hope had seen in decades had been solved, my life and organic café for people and pets had been a revolving door. I couldn't have asked for a better grand opening for *The Butler's Pantry* and hoped my mother was smiling down on me with pride. Except for one thing.

I paused, releasing a deep, cleansing breath, as tension crept back into my body.

David von Hoffster, my ex-boyfriend, had shown up, and to my dismay, had been hanging around town for the last few weeks. I'd been avoiding him at all costs. The man was relentless, which had put a slight strain on the fresh start Sheriff Chase Hargrave and I were working on. Deputy Gary Maxwell remained quietly in the background. He was an enigma I was still trying to figure out.

Out of all the men in my life, Gary was the only one who understood my need for space.

I glanced toward the cotton candy sky, trying to channel my mother's endearing presence. "I'm trying, Mom," I sighed, smiling at the memory of her shaking her head and laughing. "David needs to leave town, then my life can return to normal." I nodded once with conviction and then headed down the street toward the center of town.

At last week's charity card game, Lily Johnson, our local veterinarian, mentioned Rita had a stained glass workshop in the back of her salon. Rita Davis was our town's nail tech wizard and resident Zumba instructor. Not only were her hands magic, but she could kick your butt both into shape and at cards! She confirmed that, while it was only a hobby for now, she hoped someday she could stop painting nails and make creating art a full-time business.

Her art customers were by word of mouth only, and today I would become a client. I adjusted my prized possession held securely in a drafting tube slung over my shoulder as I checked my phone for the time. Rita and I were meeting to discuss my special project before her nail salon, *Nailed It!,* opened.

"*Ooof!*" My body collided with someone, the cap of my tube clacking onto the sidewalk. I brushed my long auburn hair out of my eyes, reminding myself to get a trim soon. "I'm so sorry," I said, glancing up in time to see Simon Banks adjust the sunglasses back across his face. From what Mrs. Bailey and Betty Henderson had told me, Simon was a traveling food blogger. Rumor had it he was still staying at the *Sunflower Inn* while his house was being built in Port Byron.

"Good morning, Juli." He bent to pick up the cap and replaced it with a firm tap back onto the tube. "Whatcha got in there? Building onto your café already?" Poor Simon, I think he needed a trim more than I did. Every time I saw him, his dark wavy hair always looked tussled, like he'd just rolled out of bed.

"Goodness no, but I do have some future plans ... in my head, of course," I corrected. Even though his face registered amusement, I couldn't see his eyes, and that somehow bothered me. As a matter of fact, I'd never seen Simon without his sunglasses. I brushed off the odd feeling of him staring at me and acknowledged he might have a light sensitivity issue or even an eye disease.

"Hmm ... if not architectural drawings, is it a photograph?" He held up his camera strapped around his neck. "I didn't know we shared the same passion."

"Not a photo. It's a canvas print. One of my favorites, and I'm having Rita create a stained glass replica for me." I peeked down at my phone for a time check. "Actually, I'm on my way to meet her now."

"Sounds fascinating. Don't let me hold you up." He waved a hand as he walked away, whistling nonchalantly. "Enjoy your day, Juli."

"You, too, Simon." I shook my head. He was an interesting character, that was for sure.

Further down the street stood *Henderson's Hardware*. Harry and Betty were outside setting out merchandise and today's sale signs. Harry stood up after strategically placing a couple seasonal garden gnomes and waved his arms in a large circle as if he didn't think I could see him. There was no mistaking Harry. He was a tall, large man with a big teddy bear, pushover personality, and his wife was the complete opposite: a petite plump woman, who was clearly in charge. I guess it was true that opposites really did attract.

There truly was no place like home. Or *gnome*, I thought to myself and held back a satisfying snort over my own cleverness.

"Well, hello there, Juli! No Major today?" Harry glanced around expecting to see Chase's sheepdog.

I shook my head. "Valerie, his regular dog walker, is back on duty. I've been demoted to backup." Which was fine by me, based on all the new business I suddenly had since my opening. I had to admit, I did miss the lovable fluff ball. But without him and Scallywag, Mrs. Bailey's feisty parrot, distracting me, I'd been able to create new tasty recipes.

"Everything okay with you and the good sheriff? I haven't seen him around much," Harry said while adjusting the sale sign. Betty waved at me before heading back inside to bring out more merchandise.

I waved back at Betty and gave Harry a shrug. "He's fine, I guess. I haven't seen him much either. Marty Thatcher retired early so Chase and Gary have been working through schedules and hoping to have a new deputy to train soon." I kind of pulled that out of nowhere and felt a little guilty about it. I mean, part of it was true. Marty did decide to take early retirement, and Chase had mentioned they were searching for a new deputy. The schedule part? That was totally made up. I had no idea what my two favorite lawmen were up to. "I love the new gnomes!" I quickly changed the subject and patted the cheerful yellow cap of the closest statue.

"They kind of grow on you." Harry chuckled, placing a hand over his stomach. "The Mrs. had the idea to order them for each season. These little fellas are part of the summer collection. I must say, they sell out fast."

"No kidding." I still wanted to stick one in Chase's front yard. Turn it into New Hope's version of Elf on a Shelf, except it would be Gnome around the Home. Oh, the hysterical places I could put one.

I reined in my childish antics when Betty reappeared. She poked her head around Harry's beefy bicep, her thick, curly blonde hair clipped up off her neck thanks to the summer heat. She fanned herself with a weekly sales flyer and said in her slight southern accent, "Oh, we don't kid about money, darlin'."

"Never!" I slapped my palm over my heart, and we all laughed.

"Where you been hidin' yourself? We didn't see you in church on Sunday." Betty turned to stack the small pile of papers in a wire rack just outside the door.

"I-I thought I was coming down with a cold, so I decide to

keep my potential germs at home." I sniffed a couple times for good measure. Yup, not only was my ticket to hell non-refundable, but I'd most likely been upgraded to first class.

Betty inspected me from head to toe. "You're lookin' fine to me."

"Ah!" I waved her off before she could detect my fib. "Must have been one of those twenty-four-hour things." I cleared my throat and was about to speak when a large trailer truck whizzed by. "Geez! They'd better slow down." My head swiveled as two more followed behind.

"Those darn carnies." Betty's face pinched in displeasure. "This happens every year when they come through."

"Carnies?" I squinted against the morning sun at the wake of dust.

"C'mon now," Harry urged. "Did you forget about the Lewis County Fair?"

"They still have that?" Suddenly I was a teenager filled with carnival excitement. Memories of candied apples, cotton candy, games, concerts, and a midway full of rides not for the faint of heart flashed through my mind.

"It's still the highlight of the summer around here." Betty stood straighter and I swear she glowed with pride.

"Is it still at the Hartman farm?" I bit my bottom lip in anticipation as ideas began to percolate for how I could promote my business.

"You betcha! Every August, going on thirty years." Harry motioned with his index finger, up and down the street. "That's why all the trucks are coming through. Thursday is the first night."

Betty crossed her arms against her ample bosom in thought. "I'm surprised Sandy Perkins didn't make you rent a booth in one of the outbuildings or a tent on the field."

"Me, too," I mused, wondering why my new-found friend forgot about me. Sandy and my mother had been huge competitors back in the day, but we had hit it off after I came back to town and her husband Bill was cleared of murder. Surely this was an oversight.

"You weren't planning on making any pies were you?" Betty asked, coming to a similar realization. "This is the first year Sandy won't be up against your mother."

"I have been so busy since my opening I didn't even know it was fair time. No worries, I will leave the pies to Sandy," I said and confirmed with a nod while I sincerely hoped she didn't leave me out on purpose. "I'll have to reach out to her." My phone buzzed in my hand. "Oops! Gotta run or I'm going to be late meeting Rita."

"All right, you take care now. Maybe you and the sheriff can tag along at the fair with April. It could be like old times." Betty clasped her hands in front of her heart, nodding rapidly as if it were a done deal.

"Maybe!" I waved and quickened my pace down the street. As much as the fair sounded like nostalgic fun, Chase and I hadn't solidified anything between us. As far as April tagging along was concerned ... that would be a nightmare waiting to happen. April was Harry and Betty's niece, and she'd been sweet on Chase since high school. While she and I seemed to find common ground after the whole *voodoo doll incident and murder accusation*, we weren't exactly besties. We never were to begin with.

Later, after touching base with Sandy, I realized I needed to contact Chase next. I suppose I had some explaining to do.

———

"It's about time!" Rita ushered me into her small studio, which was basically a decent-sized sunroom at the back of *Nailed It!* salon on Main Street, only a few blocks away from her house. The natural light coming into the room was amazing considering the time of day.

"Sorry. The Hendersons stopped me to chat. You know how they are."

"Trust me, I do. Sometimes I can't get Betty out of the chair. And when Tammy O'Toole and Sandy Perkins are in at the same time, it becomes a full-on gossip session with The Queen Belle herself, holding court." Rita flipped her silky black hair over her shoulder and held her hand in the air. Her turquoise nail polish highlighted her gorgeous Latina complexion.

"Oh, that Betty!" I knew all too well how she liked to embellish any kind of news. She loved to be the center of attention, and I wondered if that's where April got it from. I pushed the thought from my mind and shrugged. "Are you ready to see the painting?"

"Am I ever!" Rita rushed toward a large table and cleared the space, excitement radiating across her features. "Ever since you told me about it, I've been in suspense."

"So, you know art?" I asked, in awe of my friend's knowledge of more than mere manis and pedis. I opened my tube and unrolled the canvas. I longed to be able to display it at home but didn't dare, considering my method of acquisition. But a stained glass replica? No one could ever question that. I froze when Rita gasped.

"You have an Oscar Royce?" She delicately brushed her fingers on the bare edge of the canvas. Her stunned brown eyes met mine. "*Lost Horizon*."

"You know him?" Now it was my turn to be shocked.

"An old friend introduced me to his paintings many years ago." Her voice trailed off as if she were reliving a special event. "Feels like a lifetime ago." She remained quiet for a moment then shook her head. "Sorry about that. I was given his *Long Road Back* painting as a gift." She hesitated, her eyes distant, as though she were caught in the throes of the memory. "A very special gift." She appeared sorrowful, and though I was tempted to ask questions, our friendship was still too new to risk prying.

"Then you know their value?" That was a question I needed to ask. I couldn't just trust anyone with this. It meant the world to me for so many reasons. I wasn't ready to explain it all, not now—not yet.

"Of course." Rita snapped out of her melancholic stare. By the way she admired the painting, I instantly knew I could trust her. "Oscar was a street artist in Toronto and basically—"

"Rose from the ashes," we both said in unison, smiling wide as mutual recognition and respect dawned. Oscar Royce had made a name for himself with a three-dimensional apocalyptic rendering of a single rose blooming in a barren wasteland.

"So powerful." I brushed away the goosebumps prickling my arms. "His work hits on all the emotions."

"Seems you are very familiar with him, too," Rita said, settling her gaze back to the colors of the waves surrounding the burst of sky and a lighthouse. "This is more gorgeous in person. I've only seen it in magazines or online. It must have cost a fortune. He's built quite the reputation now."

I hesitated, second guessing if this was such a good idea after all.

Rita rushed over to a vintage mid-century apothecary table containing small drawers of colored materials. She balanced four in her arms and hurried back as excitement lit her eyes once more. She carefully arranged the drawers in separate quadrants on the table, their contents illuminated by the golden sunbeams streaming through the windows. "Look, these colors are perfect!"

"Wow." My mouth gaped at the different shapes of colored glass which were almost identical to the colors in Oscar's painting.

"This project was meant to be." She sifted her fingers into the drawer of ocean-colored pieces. "I'm thinking a mosaic. Or do you want it all in sheets? I have a supplier who can help with the cuts."

"Whatever you think is best. You know the artist. I trust your judgment."

"Thanks, Juli." She smiled, and I felt us bond over our love of art. "Where did you ever find this gem, anyway?"

"Oh, you might say it was one of those flash moving sales—all things must go—kind of situation."

"Crazy." Her appreciative gaze swept across the painting. "You must have gotten it for a steal."

"You have no idea." I stood there hoping she wouldn't ask more questions when suddenly her hand passed through the sunlight and my eyes were drawn to the burst of sparkle. "Rita! Is that what I think it is?" I pointed toward the oval diamond decorating her left ring finger.

"I was going to tell you when you arrived, but I was so into your painting I completely forgot!" She bounced on her toes.

"That right there, is more important than my project. When did it happen?" I grabbed her hand and admired the dazzling diamond.

"Last night. Paul took me out to our favorite hiking spot where he had already prepared the most beautiful setting at the edge of the lake."

"Sounds romantic." According to Chase, Paul Rivera owned the *Fit-Fanatics* gym in the city of Westbrook in Jefferson County. He'd been dating Rita for a couple years. We saw her with his Rottweiler, Gus, at the dog park when we took Major there.

"Paul and I grabbed take-out from the diner on our way out of town. I didn't suspect a thing."

"Take-out on a hike?" I scrunched my face in disbelief. "And you didn't suspect anything?"

"We do stuff like this all the time." She laughed. "We hike a trail, and somewhere along the way we find a rock, log or some other beautiful place to take a break and eat."

"I guess." I held my hands up in defeat. "Whatever works for you."

"I know, it seems weird, but we love to be active. When we arrived at the lake, he already had a table and chairs set up with music playing from a Bluetooth speaker. Then, as the sun set over the water, he proposed."

"How sweet." I felt tears well in my eyes as I remembered a very special dinner of my own not too long ago. I absently rubbed my bare ring finger. Something else I didn't want to talk about. Ever. I tugged at my lashes as if there were something in my eye. "I'm so happy for you. Have you guys set a date?"

"Sometime next year. We need time to plan." She held her hand out, watching the sun play off the cuts in the stone. "I still can't believe it's real." She focused back on me. "The good news is he's working with his partner on expanding their gym, *Fit-Fanatics*, and he wants to open one closer to New Hope. Then we can buy a house together somewhere in the middle."

"Oh, Rita, that's great. I know how much you love it here."

"My house is paid for thanks to my ex and our divorce settlement. I was able to buy the house mostly in cash and start the salon. I made my final mortgage payment last year."

"How awesome is that? You'll be able to sell it and practically buy the house you both want. I hear it's a seller's market out there so it's perfect timing."

"I might sell. I'm also thinking of renting it out and using some of the space to start my stained glass business if sales or my commissioned projects take off. The back of the salon is fine for now, but I will need room to display my work, kind of like a little gallery of my own with an on-site workshop."

"That's ambitious and good business sense. But I thought you were keeping it word of mouth for a while."

"I was, but Juli, your painting has made me realize how passionate I am about this. If I could show people what I can recreate, just think of the business I can gain. I've got four days before the fair starts. Right now, I'm thinking I have enough smaller pieces and some big ones I can display while using yours as a work in progress. I'm picturing this as an eighteen-by-twenty-four. What do you think?"

"That sounds perfect, but you're not going to have my painting out in the open at the fairgrounds, are you?" My insides clenched at the thought. The idea of David, or any art connoisseur—or worse, a thief—laying eyes on it made me uneasy.

"Are you crazy? Girl, people flock from all over to attend the fair. I can work from a photo if that's okay with you. But hey, no pressure. If you're not comfortable, I completely understand."

"It does make me a little nervous, but the exposure you'll have is worth it." I smiled because I meant every word. "You're so talented."

"That means so much, Juli." Rita took both of my hands. "Paul knows I'm an excellent businesswoman. I want him to see I'm thinking ahead to our future. Don't worry, I will keep your original safe and sound in my downstairs vault."

And just like that, my worry meter tripped, and I wondered if I was making the right decision after all.

Two

The humidity from the day had lifted, bringing a gentle breeze as the sun was setting. I'd changed my faded denim cutoffs for a pair of olive-green, wide leg capri pants and a white cropped tank. Comfort and style. Chase planned on grilling fish for dinner. Even though I was a vegetarian, I had been known to dip my toes in the pescatarian pond now and then.

"Why didn't you tell me it was Lewis County Fair time?" I asked while carrying the bottle of white wine and two glasses onto Chase's two-tier deck, made from dark grey composite material which complemented the dark blue siding of his house. I acknowledged the shaggy sheepdog with kissing noises and a pat on his head once I set the items on the tiled tabletop. Grabbing the lighter, I then proceeded to light the strategically placed citronella candles.

"We haven't exactly been in the same space to have any kind of conversation." He placed the salmon smoothly on the grill. "Almost makes me think you've been avoiding me on purpose." I caught the almost teasing side eye as he adjusted the heat.

"About that." I avoided his watchful eyes by focusing on a ladybug creeping across the table.

"Were you?" His mustache twitched.

"Not entirely." I poured the wine, feeling the heat of his scrutiny. "Believe it or not I've been baking new treats and creating custom orders. I've had to hire additional servers so they will be fully trained when Andie and Scott go back to school." I handed him a glass then took a seat at the table while he tended to the grill.

Andie Evans was Jimmy and Tammy O'Toole's niece who had come to stay with them after getting mixed up with the wrong set of friends in Detroit. I hired her as a barista, and she was a natural. Come to find out, she'd grown up with Scott Iverson. Scott worked part time at *Ringo's Diner*, and I'd convinced him to take on some hours with me at *Petite Four Paws Café*. Scott and Andie were going into their senior year and had been dating for about a month, thanks to my stealthy matchmaking skills.

"Sounds like being an entrepreneur suits you. I'm happy for you, Julianna, I really am," he said while walking toward the table.

"But?" I had to ask, if only to take my mind off the fact that his rock band T-shirt hugged his upper body in all the right places, not to mention how well he filled out a pair of basketball shorts.

"I never should have doubted you."

"Wait a minute," I said as I jumped up and placed my hand on his forehead. "Are you feeling okay?" I moved my palm across his skin to check the temperature at his cheeks.

"I'm fine." He removed my hand but continued to hold it within his. His green eyes twinkled and a warmth spread up my arm until I felt the flush reach my own cheeks.

"I'll need that statement in writing, Officer." I slipped my hand away and tipped my glass for a longer sip.

"That I'm fine?" He opened his arms wide. "I think you can see that for yourself." He moved in a slow circle, giving me ample time to appreciate how incredibly fine and fit he was while he strutted his way back toward the grill. My tongue moistened my parched lips, and I swallowed hard when he glanced over his shoulder at me.

"Very funny." I approached the grill to avoid making a fool of myself. He stayed quiet and I watched him tend to our meal until I could find my voice. "Seriously, I do appreciate it." I nudged his hip. "What you said. It means a lot for you to believe in me."

"I know. But it doesn't explain why you've stayed away. We're ... neighbors, after all." He kept his attention on the sizzling salmon and my heart dipped a little.

"Is that all?" The soft-spoken question hung in the air, and I wondered if he'd taken my space to mean I didn't want to explore what was still there. To my surprise, he gently closed the grill and turned to face me.

"Why don't you tell me."

"I-I'm not sure."

"And there you have it."

"Chase, wait." I grabbed his arm as he started to turn away. "There's so much on my mind and I don't know where to start. I've just been on my own for so long, it's difficult for me to trust someone fully. Every time I have, I've gotten burned." I swallowed my fear. "I want to see where this goes, please believe that."

"I can do that." He kept his eyes trained on me. "Don't keep things from me, Julianna. We've been down that road before and I don't think we need a replay, considering how that turned out."

"Of course. You're absolutely right." Oh boy. I knew I needed to come clean about David, but now was not the time. I felt as if we were still on shaky ground. Our foundation needed to be steady before I threw David von Hoffster at him. "So, how's the search for the new deputy going?"

"Way to change the subject, Scarlett." He chuckled, and I relaxed, finding comfort in the nickname he'd chosen for me when we were kids. "It's going well. Gary knows a couple guys who are ready for small town life."

"Really? Has he told them the truth about New Hope?" I winked, then drained my glass. "Hold that thought I need to grab the asparagus." Moments later, I returned with a foil pouch containing asparagus seasoned with a little garlic, salt and pepper. Chase opened the cover, and I set it on the top rack of the grill. "When does the new rookie arrive?"

Chase refilled my glass, and I clinked it against his. "You watch too many reality shows. We haven't hired anyone yet. Gary is only asking those who have said they'd like to get out of the city."

"Meet a little country girl and settle down?" I immediately thought of April and wondered if she'd even let a new lawman into her life. Maybe I needed to pray on that in church if I ever wanted to move forward. "Oh, and for the record, my life has been enough of a reality show. TV is off limits."

"Nice lead in. Care to elaborate?"

"I really need to get my off button fixed." I sighed, frustrated with myself.

"Your what?" He squinted at me, and scratched his five o'clock shadow. "You know, never mind. Our dinner is ready."

"Saved by the salmon!" I joyously yelled and joined him at the table where he plated up the salmon and veggies. "This is perfection," I said after my first bite of fish.

"Glad you like it." He cleared his throat and the mischief in his eyes clouded with something serious. I swallowed hard as I watched Chase seem to struggle to find the right words. "I want you to know—"

"Juuuli."

We whipped our necks around to see Scallywag, sweet Mrs. Bailey's big blue parrot, bobbing his plumed head high up in the maple tree. Major began to bark and jump against the base of the trunk, as if the big lug thought he could catch him. Just to tease the pile of fluff more, Scallywag swooped from the limb right toward the dog's head, a flurry of leaves falling in his wake. More than ready to protect his yard, Major launched himself into the air, intercepting the devilish bird.

"Oh no!" I jumped from my seat, followed by Chase.

"Major!" he commanded. The dog sat proudly with a few blue

feathers hanging out of his mouth. The bird, no worse for wear, perched on the edge of the fence, wings flapping and angrily squawking. "Does he look injured?" Chase questioned, taking his eyes off his dog long enough to look at me.

"I'm not going anywhere near him right now. I've never seen that bird so angry." I stepped away from the fence.

"Juli, Juli, oh no, Juuuli!" the bird called as he flew over the rooftop.

"That naughty bird." I turned my attention to Major. "You're kind of a good boy, but also a little naughty." Major whined and sat next to me while I removed the feathers. "That crazy fowl is not going to taste like chicken so get that right out of your fuzzy head."

"Where's Mrs. Bailey tonight?"

"She's at her Tuesday quilting circle with her sister in Williamsville. She won't be home 'til tomorrow morning."

Chase sighed dramatically and set his fork down. "Which means we need to catch that bird."

"Just like old times." I waggled my brows, seeing the sparkle in his eyes. "You up for it?"

Chase smiled wide, rubbing his hands together in anticipation of the adventure. "Heck yeah, I'll grab the pillowcase. Let's go!"

It took us two hours, half a box of sesame peeps and countless foiled attempts before we outsmarted the precocious parrot. I used the spare key Mrs. B had given me, while Chase followed with a pillowcase full of an agitated Scallywag. He deposited the bird back in his giant brass cage, and I tossed in a couple more peeps for good measure.

"Juli bad," Scallywag said in a low tone. "Baaad, Juli."

"He's got plenty of food and water. I wonder why he escaped," Chase said, taking a closer look around the cage. "And what's his hang up with you?"

"Probably heard us and Major. He must get lonely when Mrs. B isn't here to talk to him." I glared at the bird. "Who knows? He's probably jealous of Major."

"I'm glad Mrs. Bailey gets out and about. I was a little worried about her after my parents moved to Florida and then your mom died." He paused and I looked away as the frequent lump in my throat returned. "Hey, I'm sorry." His fingers guided my chin back to face him.

"It's okay. I miss her every day, Chase. I wish I'd called her more. I wish I'd come to visit or had her come to see me. I wish she could see that I'm finally ..." The sob broke free.

Chase drew me into his arms. "She knew, Julianna. Don't ever doubt that. She told everyone how proud she was of you."

"That's what Mrs. Bailey told me," I said with my face buried in his shirt.

"It's true." He tipped my head back and wiped my tears then draped the blanket over Scallywag's cage. "Let's leave before this bird gets into more trouble."

"Trouuuble, click-click-click," cooed Scallywag from under the blanket, "coming your way."

"What's he clucking about now?" Chase kept his voice low as we made our way to the door.

I shrugged and locked up, but couldn't stop the nagging sensation of pending doom from forming in my gut.

We walked back to Chase's house to find a major disaster. We'd been in such a hurry to catch Scallywag, we'd forgotten to pick up our plates and close the patio door. There was Major, sprawled on the kitchen floor with his furry face covered in salmon. On the deck there were two broken plates and an empty foil pouch.

"Guilty as charged, mister." Chase pointed a finger. "Outside until I can clean this mess up." The dog hung his head, ears drooping, and plodded out to the yard. His steps were slow and heavy, each one a reluctant surrender.

"I can help." I grabbed a roll of paper towels.

"Nah, I got this." He placed his hand over mine and the familiar comfort that was us washed over me.

"I know," I said in a whisper. "You always do." Right then and there I wanted to pour it all out. Chase, me, David. I needed him to know everything, to understand, to know that ...

"Julianna." The soft, yet commanding tone of his voice sent a thrill through my body I hadn't felt in a very long time. I felt his breath on my skin as his face dipped toward mine. I wanted to speak but no words were needed when our eyes met and mine slowly closed.

I'll tell him later.

"Woof-Woof-Woof!" In an instant, Major pushed himself between us.

"Major!" we both cried out, surprised by the canine intervention.

"What has gotten into him?" Chase held two fuzzy front paws and plopped him gently on the ground.

"Remember what Lily Johnson said the last time I brought him to her vet clinic?" I glanced from my fluffy buddy to his master. "He needs quality time. You've been busy and tonight was waylaid by Mr. Scallywag. I'm sure the big boy wants your attention."

"You're probably right." Chase sighed.

"I'll see myself out." I patted Major's head. "Thank you for earlier." I glanced up from under my lashes, suddenly feeling embarrassed.

"Always." He smiled and I caught a twinkle in his deep green eyes. "How about we have a do-over? I'll take you to the Fair on Thursday night. Gary's taking the night shift so I'm all yours."

"Sounds great. It's been a long time."

I walked home, finding solace in the deep bond Chase and I shared. We had a lifetime of history. That's what made our relationship so comfortable. I looked forward to uninterrupted time together. Putting my key in the lock, I turned the knob, pausing when I heard Scallywag.

"Troubles coming! Click-Click-Click."

"You don't know what you're talking about," I said toward

Mrs. Bailey's house and closed my door. Only my worry meter rose a couple notches, making me double-check my doors and windows just in case the crazy bird was right.

―――――

OPENING NIGHT OF THE LEWIS COUNTY FAIR AND THE field was a sea of people. The crowds, the food smells, and screams from the midway all felt like home. I'd spoken to Sandy Perkins who apologized for her error. She'd given me tent space right next to Rita and her stained glass tent. Andie Evans and Scott Iverson happily agreed to run my tent until eight o'clock each night, with Betty and Tammy O'Toole filling in during the day while they took a lunch break. I was grateful for some time away from the kitchen and promised to check in throughout each day of the fair.

"Please tell me Bilal's Falafel Oasis is still here," I groaned with impending hunger as Chase and I walked toward the midway and the variety of food trucks intentionally placed around the field. I'd purposely skipped lunch, knowing I'd be tasting my way through the night.

"It's still here. I take it that's where we're starting?" He held out his hand, and I didn't hesitate to hold it.

"No one makes tabbouleh salad like Bilal. Not even my friend, Oliver, who happens to be a magnificent chef in Boston." I smiled, dragging Chase along as I thought of my Boston crew. I hoped they were all right, now that David was darkening my doorstep and leaving them alone. I had yet to reach out, not sure how they would feel hearing from me.

"I look forward to meeting them sometime." Chase's voice pulled me from my thoughts, and I slowed down. "I'm surprised they weren't here for your grand opening."

"They wanted to be, but there was a lot going on. Nando and Amelia help with Ollie's catering business."

"Ah, I see." Chase studied me and I couldn't tell if he waited for me to elaborate or if he was okay with my answer. Thankfully, I didn't have to respond.

"Who's that talking to Simon?" I asked, discreetly pointing toward a dark-haired man with the broadest shoulders and biggest biceps I'd ever seen. The man could have been a Greek God without the mane of golden hair. "He doesn't look very happy."

"You can put your eyes back in your head, Scarlett, that's Paul Rivera. He's Rita's boyfriend, the guy that owns the Rottie from the dog park."

"That is Rita's Paul?" I stared, mouth agape, envisioning the gorgeous couple together doing all the crazy fitness activities they loved. "You weren't kidding when you called them a power couple."

"Yeah, the two of them together are a regular smoke show."

"And by them, you mean Rita?"

"I forget you're such a comedian." Chase shook his head in his usual exasperation and turned his gaze back toward Simon. "I don't know Paul very well, but whenever he's been in town with Rita, he's struck me as a pretty levelheaded guy."

"Well, you'll get to know him more because he and Rita got engaged!" My excitement vanished with Chase's shocked expression, and I clasped my hand over my mouth. "On second thought, you didn't hear that from me."

"That's good news, isn't it?"

"Of course it is, I'm just not sure if I should be the one spreading the word."

"Don't worry, your secrets are always safe with me." Chase draped his arm across my shoulders, leading me in the opposite direction, but not before I caught the distinct furrow of his brows. "Let's get you your taboo salad."

"It's tabbouleh, and you should give it a try."

"That's all you, sweetheart."

The endearment caught me off guard, especially after the mention of my secrets. I exhaled a big breath, causing him to pull me a little closer. Again, my conscience kicked me to come clean. If not now, when?

"Juli! Chase!" A man with a larger-than-life personality rushed from the nearest food truck. Immediately I knew we'd arrived at the Falafel Oasis.

"Hey, Sam!" Chase released me and clasped Samir Rahmani in a bro-hug of sorts. "How the heck are you?"

"Sam, oh my gosh! It's been years." I gave him a hug and he kissed my cheek. "Are you working for your dad?"

"I know, it's been a long time." He grinned from ear to ear, cocoa eyes sparking with sheer happiness. "I left for Weill Cornell Medical College in Qatar and haven't had a chance to come back because I've also been caring for my jiddo until my cousin's job transfer came through."

"I hope your grandfather is well. Are you here to stay now?" Chase eagerly asked. I'm sure he was ready to add more eligible bachelors to New Hope's pool to take the pressure off himself.

"Only for the summer, my friend. But I won't be so far away this time. I started my fellowship in Forensic Pathology in New York City."

"That's fantastic."

"What would be fantastic," Bilal Rahmani stuck his silvered head out from the back of the truck, "is my long-lost son coming back in here to cook. Do you see that line? We have customers!"

"Ah, Baba, I am coming!" Sam patted Chase on the back. "We'll catch up soon, the three of us, like we used to do."

"Sounds good, Sam." Chase gave a firm handshake, and we waved as Sam rushed inside the truck. "This line is huge, are you sure you want to wait around?" He pointed to the line which had grown since we'd been chatting.

"I think we're going to wait no matter where we go. I'm okay going somewhere else, but I'm bringing you back here even if we need to come back tomorrow."

"Deal."

"Why are you being so agreeable? Are you sure you're not sick?" I inspected him from head to toe just as Betty had done to me.

"You ask too many questions."

"Don't you ever get tired of being a sheriff?"

"Again—"

"For goodness sakes, can we *please* find something to eat." I yanked him in a different direction, not sure what we were going to find, but my empty stomach wasn't about to wait. Hearing Chase's laughter brought me peace when thinking about what our next steps were going to look like. "Look! Dairy-free nachos!"

"On a dairy farm?"

"We've got to try them. This just makes me more confident in the success of *The Butler's Pantry*, oh, lawman of little faith." I shook my finger in front of his nose. "People are becoming more conscious of what they put in their bodies."

"I apologized, remember? I'm a changed man." The grin pulling at his cheeks kept me firmly in our comfort zone.

"Face it, Sheriff, I'm trending." Comfort was good, I reminded myself. I didn't need dangerous or adventurous. All either had ever done was get me into trouble.

"If you say so. Why don't you go get your fake nachos, and *maybe* I'll try one."

"I'll make you a believer yet." I pulled some cash from my cross-body purse and froze at the sight of something very familiar over Chase's left shoulder. Partially hidden in the crowd was the brim of a hat the color of ink. I knew it was a fedora even before he came into full view. The sleek, familiar silhouette sent a chill down my spine. I swallowed the small bubble of fear in my throat. It couldn't be.

Had Eddie followed David to New Hope?

Eddie Costello was the last person I thought I'd see. One of the few I never cared to see again. Another skeleton who needed to go away.

"Juli, did you hear me? I said don't forget the jalapeños."

"What?" I blinked rapidly before focusing on Chase's puzzled expression. "On second thought, let's hit the midway." I began pulling him towards the rides when he planted his feet, causing me to rebound against him.

"What happened to being starving?" The playful twinkle in his eyes and most adorable smile did nothing to ease my growing panic. I didn't like David sticking around town, and now Eddie had shown up. My worry meter engaged, and I was not going to ignore it.

"I am. But so is everyone else. I bet there won't be long lines yet on the midway, and if we don't have food in our stomachs, we won't get sick on all the spinning rides."

"We've never gotten sick. Why are you acting so weird?"

I ignored his question and dragged him to an empty line. "Look! How about this one?"

"You hate the Ferris wheel."

"I used to." I glanced around, hoping Chase didn't notice my anxiety. "It's been so long, and I want to see all the views as it goes around."

The carnival worker tipped his ball cap and opened the bar to the seat. "Sheriff."

"After you, Scarlett." Chase waved me forward and we both sat down. With a snap of the bar, we were in motion. "I thought you liked this ride," he said while leaning back, which made the bucket rock and my muscles clench.

"I do. This is great." I tried to scan the ground for Eddie, but the ride had picked up speed. "I love the wind in my face."

"Then why don't you loosen your grip." Chase pried my white-knuckled fingers from the safety bar. I presented him with a sheepish grin then raised my chin a notch to show I wasn't afraid of the ride. My fear stemmed from something else.

"Safety first, Officer Do-Good. Besides, it's been years since

I've been on one of these things. I don't remember it going so fast."

"Don't worry, I've got you." In one smooth motion he brought his arm around my shoulders and drew me closer.

I leaned into him, watching the colors of the fair and views of the surrounding countryside swirl in and out of sight. Relaxing against Chase had me wondering if maybe I'd imagined Eddie's inky fedora. With the massive crowds at the County Fair, it could have been anyone, and I was content to leave it at that. As for David, he needed to leave town quickly and take all his triggering memories with him. My fresh start had just begun, and I didn't want any interruptions or distractions.

That's when the ride came to a jolting stop.

Three

"What just happened." My heart began to race when I realized we were stuck at the very top of the Ferris wheel. My least favorite spot to be. The sky had turned to dusk, creating the perfect backdrop for the bright lights and midway excitement.

"I don't know." Chase leaned to the right trying to look over the side of our bucket. "That sounded mechanical. And I don't see Clive Huntley."

"Who's that and can they get us down?" I could almost feel myself hyperventilating.

"He's the guy running the ride, so yes he can ... whenever he gets back." Chase settled back into the seat.

"Whenever he gets back?" I repeated, my vocal cords strained when I reached my ultimate high. "Did he forget we were on the ride? Who vacates their post for a midway ride, anyway?"

"I certainly hope he didn't forget. I'd have to write him up, and he's a good man, comes every year."

I swatted his arm. "You'd better be teasing me."

He shrugged, unbothered by my juvenile outburst. "While we're waiting, why don't you tell me what you're up to?"

"Me?" I pointed to myself. "I'm not up to anything, except maybe a thousand feet in the air about to die."

"We're *maybe* sixty or seventy feet up. And you're not going to die."

"You can't guarantee that."

"What I can assure you of is how nervous you were down there. Clearly, someone or something has rattled you." He hesitated as I gaped at him in disbelief. "Remember, I'm a trained professional."

My lips pursed as I struggled to come up with something to say. While I had planned on confessing about David, Eddie's potential involvement added a complicated twist that Chase didn't need to know. Keeping this secret buried forever seemed like the only option. "How could I ever forget," I managed to say.

"Is there something going on you're afraid to tell me?" His sudden shift in the seat made my heart race, and I gripped the bar tightly. "Look at me." I wanted to tell him everything, but fear and doubt held me back, keeping me stuck in silence.

"Stop rocking us, or we're going to flip. You know how I hate this ride." I pinched my eyes tight at my own admission. Peeking under my lashes, I caught his cheesy grin.

"I know."

My eyes sprang open. "And you let me do this anyway?"

"I figured you had your reasons." He paused, then added, "Now would be a good time to tell me."

I didn't want to upset Chase with what I had to say. Growing up, he always brushed things off easily, but I couldn't be sure if he still had that same resilience. Despite knowing that David and I were over for good, I couldn't shake the feeling of guilt and uncertainty about how Chase would react. I stayed quiet for a moment in my feelings. The evening air had cooled the day, and sitting on top of the world with him, ready to bear my soul, felt one hundred percent right.

"Okay." I smiled then almost laughed at his wide-eyed expression.

A mix of surprise and intrigue flickered across his face. He gave a small, almost imperceptible nod, acknowledging my affirmation. "Wasn't expecting that."

"Uhm ... I don't think you're expecting a crowd down below either. What do you think is going on?" I pointed to the mass of people gathering around the ride. "Is that someone on the ground? Chase, I think it's a fight."

We both leaned as far as we dared to get a better look. I sucked in a breath when the bucket tipped too far forward. We both sat back, and my heart pounded with each rocking tilt.

"Let's not do that again," I panted.

"I need to get down there. It looks like Clive might have gotten hurt."

"Hey! Sheriff! Remember us? Now whose got the last laugh?" A burly young man slapped his chest then teetered back a couple steps. The other young man caught him before he fell completely, then handed him a plastic cup of what looked like beer. "How's it feel to be helpless, huh Sheriff?"

"That's right!" The other man chimed in, holding his cup of beer high for us to see. "Next time think twice about writing us a ticket when we were just having fun."

I turned my eyes on Chase. "Oh dear, another free spirit you tried to lock up. What did I tell you about tossing the rule book?" I tsked.

He scowled. "Not now, Juli." He fidgeted in our seat like a caged tiger needing to be free. "The Ross brothers. Josh and James. They like to joy ride late at night. We've been getting complaints about cars racing. Gary and I stopped them last week. Of course, they'd also been drinking, so not the sharpest tools in the shed. We let them sober up in a jail cell overnight. Their parents weren't amused either."

"Yikes. From the looks of things below, those boys haven't learned a lesson."

With one loud "clunk," the Ferris wheel began moving once again. When we got to the bottom, Gary stopped the giant wheel and opened our lock.

"Thanks, Gary!" I flashed an overly exaggerated smile primarily to diffuse Chase, but it didn't work.

"Of course. Nice to see you again, Juli."

"What happened to Clive and where did the Ross brothers go?" Chase stormed off the platform with me and Gary right behind. The crowd had disbursed, and Clive sat on a stool with and small bag of ice on his head. "Clive, are you okay?"

"Just fine, Sheriff. Those dang fellas had a bit too much to drink, pushing and shoving each other. We've got a record crowd here for opening night, you know. Anyway, one of them rammed into me, and I fell into the control panel and blacked out."

"Yeah, someone called it in to the EMT station, and I got a call." Gary handed Clive a bottle of water.

"You taking them in?" Chase sounded all business, even without the uniform.

"I got Marty to come into the station so I could bring Liam with me," Gary replied. "He's back at the car with the brothers." Gary reached for Chase's arm as he turned to leave. "Stay here and enjoy the night, Boss. We've got everything under control."

I watched the tension in Chase's features. Those boys had made it personal, and I wondered if New Hope's prized lawman would be able to let this one go. He locked eyes with me, and I grinned, cocking my head in hopes he'd make the correct choice. The insufferable man kept me in suspense longer than necessary. Just as my brows pinched together in irritation, he winked and turned back to Gary.

"Fine. But they stay overnight, I don't care what their parents say. They don't own this town."

"Neither do you," I mumbled as I gnawed my cuticle.

"Juli ..." he warned.

"I'm on it, Boss." Gary nodded toward me, "Juli." Putting an arm around the older man's shoulders, he said, "C'mon Clive, let's get you home. Looks like your replacement just got here."

"Well, Sheriff, do you want to try another ride?" I looped my arm through his, and he grumbled something inaudible. "Don't let those hooligans ruin our night."

"*Our* night. I like the sounds of that."

And there it was, that familiar flutter in my chest that had returned the moment I came back to town. Mom used to tell me to watch for signs whenever I was torn in making an important decision. My best friend in Boston, Amelia, always told me the heart doesn't lie. This time, I tended to believe her.

"Me too," I said, and meant every word. But that didn't stop my worry meter from humming a warning, and I refused to believe that psycho parrot was right.

———

"CHASE! JULI! WAIT UP!" A TRILLING VOICE CALLED, crashing through my happiness vibe like a pair of giant cymbals.

April Henderson.

I raised hopeful eyes toward our common denominator. "Do we have to?" No doubt she wanted Chase to see her in all her perky glory, dressed in some sort of matching outfit meant to get his attention. He slowed our pace, and I sighed loudly, already knowing the answer.

"Wait up a sec!" she called out once more and we stopped.

"Be nice," he said before he laughed. "I have faith in you." He released my hand and turned. "April, how are you?" Chase opened his arms for a hug, and she couldn't have rushed in fast enough.

"So much better, now." She pressed herself tight to him, and I didn't miss the sly smile spreading across her face before she buried it into his shoulder. The groan escaped my lips louder than intended, and Chase lifted a hand from her back long enough to waggle a finger at me.

I groaned again for good measure.

"What brings you out tonight?" I crossed my arms and rocked back on the heels of my sneakers. April wore a purple floral sundress and grey cowboy boots, looking all country-cute compared to my white denim shorts, Celtics t-shirt and high-tops. "You just missed Chase and I being stuck at the top of the Ferris wheel." When she didn't move, I added, "Alone. At the top."

April pulled back, her eyes wide, and I winked. The hook had been set. *Sorry Mom.*

"Oh." She smoothed the front of her dress and flipped her braid over to the other shoulder. "Glad you're down or I'd never have found you. Aunt Betty said I should hurry to the fairgrounds and catch up with you guys." She giggled. "Well, look at us, it's just like old times."

"Except Chase and I—"

"Are so glad you're here," Chase finished my sentence, not the way I planned it at all. "Isn't that right, Juli?"

"Right." I clenched my teeth until my jaw ached. Leave it to Sheriff Do-Good. So much for *our* night. April had a way of bringing me right back to high school, reminding me of why I'd left after graduation in the first place.

"So where are we headed? Did you guys eat? Maybe we should hit up one of the rides. We'll all fit in the spinning barrels, or maybe the flying swing seats." April's eyes lit with excitement. I'm sure she was envisioning a ride where Chase was between us. Since I had last asked the question before we were interrupted, I cast a longing, hopeful gaze toward Chase. When he didn't take the lead, I jumped in.

"Definitely had our fill of the Ferris wheel. It's up to you," I deferred to Chase, putting him purposely on the spot. "What would be your choice for our night together." There, I'd said it, put it out for the universe and April Henderson to hear. She took a step back as an unforeseen reality dawned. Chase's gorgeous eyes flashed with surprise, then recognition of what I had just verbally solidified. His hand slipped into mine, and he gave a reassuring squeeze.

"Flying swings." His eyes never left mine.

"Great choice." My heart quickened its rhythm.

"I know."

"C'mon guys, the ride just let out, maybe we can find seats together." April rushed ahead while we took our time. The comfortable silence between us speaking volumes to where we were headed. As we passed through the gate, I noticed April had already found a row of three. She sat on the outside swing. I pretended I didn't see her and pulled Chase toward the opposite side of the ride.

"Right here." I grabbed the middle seat and held the chain for the outside seat.

"What about April?"

"She's fine where she is. If this is seriously our night, I don't want April interfering." I buckled the safety chain across my waist and between my legs.

Chase did the same. "She's not interfering. She's a friend hanging out."

"Stop drinking the Kool-Aid. If we had a fight right now, she would swoop in just like she did before."

"Don't you think after the last few weeks she knows things are different?" The ride started up and he took my hand as we slowly went in a circle, increasing altitude and speed.

"She does now," I yelled against the breeze in our faces. When I glanced at Chase, he was shaking his head and laughing.

When the ride stopped, we met back up with April. My stomach announced its anger over still not being fed. We decided to head back to the food truck court after snagging a blue and green cloud of cotton candy.

I had to admit, it did feel just like old times. Chase and I, hands still joined, our future path forming with each step. Nothing was going to stop us now. My overactive imagination had been for nothing.

Four

"Look, there's Rita's stained glass booth. Let's go and say hello." I led Chase and April toward the tent. "I need to check in on Andie and Scott, too." Opening night, I wanted them to stay later. Once the weekend hit, I told them they could close at six o'clock and go have fun.

"Hi guys!" Rita smiled proudly over all her creations and the beginning of my project laying on a worktable in the back.

"I hear congratulations are in order," Chase said as Rita exited the tent.

"Thank you. We're very excited about this next journey in our lives."

"Change is good," I added.

"Wait, did I miss something?" April inserted herself into the conversation, flanking Chase's other side.

"Paul and I are engaged." Rita extended her hand.

April gasped and Chase let loose a low whistle.

"I'm so happy for you!" April bounced forward and hugged Rita.

"Thank you," she said, pulling away to glance up and down the rows of tents. "I'm waiting for Paul to get here. He's got a huge tent to promote *Fit-Fanatics*, closer to the Grande Court. They are having a bodybuilding competition on Saturday afternoon. He's competing and has clients he's been training who are competing. It's going to be great for his business."

"Maybe we can all grab a bite to eat together. I'm starving." I rubbed my stomach, eager to keep moving toward the Falafel Oasis.

"You're the one who insisted on the rides, remember?" Chase teased.

"Oh, here he comes!" Rita broke in, waving her arm high as Paul approached.

I had yet to meet Paul Rivera. At a distance he seemed good looking and fit. Up close, it was a whole new ball game. The man was ripped and cut in ways that should be illegal. Seeing him and Rita side by side, they were a united force to be reckoned with. Rita only came up to his shoulders and even her super fit body seemed petite against all his muscle. Both had striking Latino features.

I was in awe.

"Everyone, this is Paul, my fiancé." Rita beamed, and he kissed her cheek before flashing a bright smile and a wave. She frowned. "Baby, you look tired. Do you need a snack? When was the last time you checked your sugar?"

"Eh, I'm fine. You worry too much." He affectionately rubbed the center of her back. "You know me, I had to sample all the varieties of foods here. I've never heard of some of these businesses. I think I ate a little too much."

"How many times do I have to tell you, if you're going to eat without thinking, then you need to make sure you have your insulin with you. Do you have it?" She crossed her arms and tapped her foot against the solid ground.

"It's back at my tent. I'm fine. Just thirsty."

"Let me grab you a water," I said, springing into action.

"It's in the cooler in the corner," Rita called as I jogged into her tent. I appeared a moment later with two bottles.

"Well, well, what do we have here?" said the familiar voice from my past. I whipped around to see David von Hoffster infiltrating into our cozy group. He was dressed more for a polo match than a county fair, with his khaki pants, leather shoes, white dress shirt and linen jacket. Not a hair was out of place, and his smile remained full of the charm he was known for. "Hello, Rita, darling. It's been a while."

"David?" The name hung in the air like a half-forgotten spell. The color drained from Rita's face, leaving her as pale as a ghost. I suddenly wondered if she'd been hiding skeletons too?

My worry meter kicked in gear, and a gnawing sensation churned within my gut. Something wasn't right. I swallowed a mouthful of air, the uneasy feeling of deeply buried secrets clawing their way to the surface.

"Rita?" Her name slipped from my lips, a lifeline in a sea of unease.

I barely heard Chase ask softly, "What's going on?"

David stepped forward, commanding attention. "I couldn't help but overhear your joyous news as I walked by."

"Who the hell are you?" Paul positioned himself in front of Rita, hands fisted as if he'd sensed the same disruptive energy as me.

"David von Hoffster. And I'm afraid I have some news of my own." David pulled a legal-size piece of paper from the inside of his linen suit pocket. I prayed he was about to share that he just bought an island in the Caribbean and was leaving tonight.

"What could you possibly have to say?" Rita's deep brown eyes were like daggers aimed directly at David as she stood united with Paul. Something sinister was definitely brewing beneath the surface.

"Dearest Rita. I hate to be the one raining on your happy little parade, but you're not marrying Mr. Muscle over here."

"What are you talking about?" Paul stood taller, sticking his chest out in defiance.

My skin prickled as Chase stepped closer, ready to break up whatever was about to happen.

"She can't marry you because she is still married to me."

"What?" Rita and I exclaimed together.

"I signed that paperwork years ago. I even received a settlement after our divorce was final. Why are you doing this to me?" Rita might have sounded tough, but I caught the glint of a tear at the corner of her eye.

"I know you signed it. I sent you the settlement money from my personal account." He sighed, as if he'd performed a miracle we should all be grateful for.

The cotton candy I'd recently ingested fermented in my empty stomach as the drama continued.

"Why would you do that?" Rita posed the question on all our minds. "Why didn't you give it to the lawyer?"

"I was heading out the door for a month abroad with every intention of turning it in when I got back. I didn't want you to have to wait for it all to be processed. Besides, you know how business works in the art world. Things picked up once I returned and I completely forgot. I didn't think it was a big deal."

"Not a big deal?" Rita shrieked. "I wanted to be done with you, David. I have moved on, and I'm in love with Paul. You have no control over what I do anymore."

"Wait a minute!" I held up my hand, my heart thundering in my chest over her words. Blindly stepping forward, I pushed through the memories that threatened to suffocate me. "You were married to Rita when you proposed to me?"

"You ..." The air left Rita's lungs in a gasp.

"Were engaged to *him*?" Chase's voice sliced through the air as he finished Rita's sentence. I whipped around so fast I almost fell. The pain in his eyes from my unintentional confession crushed my heart.

"Oh, Chase, no." My voice came out as a whisper, but he didn't move closer. When I stepped back beside him, he recoiled as if my touch would burn him.

"You son of a ..." Paul surged forward with a right cross into David's face. David remained on his feet and returned a blow to Paul's ribs. Rita screamed but Paul pushed her away as he pummeled David again with two jabs and an uppercut.

"That's enough!" Chase pushed between the two men; their arms locked around each other's necks. "Stand down." He gave David a shove in one direction and slung Paul toward Rita where she grabbed his bicep to hold him back.

"It was an honest mistake, Sheriff," David spoke between gulps of air. "Rita, I thought you should know in case you wanted to change your mind." David gazed at Rita with an expression I'd never seen before.

It appeared he still had feelings for her. I knew it shouldn't bother me, but it did. All the time we'd spent together, and I'd pushed away feelings for Chase, I should have been listening to my own heart.

"I'm not changing my mind. You need to file those records now because Paul and I are getting married next year, and I want you scratched from my life forever."

"I think you have your answer, David." Chase acknowledged my ex with zero emotion on his face, fully in sheriff mode. I knew I'd hurt him and with all the tension swirling in the air I wondered what he had in store for me. "Why don't you head back to wherever it is you're staying."

"Better yet, go back to Boston," I announced. All eyes trained on me, holding the remaining cotton candy in my hands. "What? He doesn't belong here."

"Oh, but I do, Julianna. And you know why."

"We're done here," Chase commanded. "If I see or hear about either of you fighting again, you'll both be sitting in a holding pen with the rest of the delinquents. Now go home."

Chase turned and walked past me; the tension formed a barrier between us I wasn't sure how to navigate. I'd been blindsided as much as everyone else. I regretted more than ever not telling him about David on the Ferris wheel, or at dinner, or during my grand opening. He had every right to know, and now I may have ruined everything.

Then again, this was me and Chase. We were stronger than anything David could dish out. I knew exactly who and what he was, and I wasn't about to let him get under my skin again. The man was an all-around liar, he'd just proven that fact.

"I bet you could use a burger right about now, huh?" I elbowed him in the ribs, trying to lighten the mood.

"Not hungry."

"What about the Falafel Oasis?"

"I think it's best if I take you home. Sam sent a text and wants to meet us for coffee at *Ringo's* first thing in the morning."

"Okay. We can still get something to eat."

"Not tonight, Julianna." He kept his tone short and didn't say another word until we got home.

I followed him up the creaky steps of his front porch, the wood groaning beneath our weight. Every unspoken word hung in the cool night air. I hated the silent treatment, but I also didn't know what to say. I'd had a full life away from New Hope. Why didn't I think he was going to understand that?

"What are you doing?" he asked, his voice startling cold as he turned the key in the lock. From inside the house, Major barked, a sharp sound that echoed the tension between us.

"I thought I'd come in," I said, my voice barely above a whisper.

"I don't think that's a good idea," he replied, the finality in his tone sending a shiver down my spine.

"But I—"

"Have something you want to tell me?" He turned fully to face me, and for the first time he didn't resemble the man I had known since forever. Gone was the playful spark in his eyes, replaced by something much more foreboding, which swept a chill across my skin like the first fall breeze.

"I—" I began, but the words caught in my throat.

"I knew you were holding something back. What I don't understand is why you couldn't tell me," he said, his eyes boring into mine with an intensity that made my heart ache.

"Chase, I wanted to but—"

"But you didn't," he cut in, his voice hard and unyielding. "Which leads me to believe there's more you're not telling me."

We stood in silence, the porch light casting long shadows that danced around us. I wanted to explain, to bridge the gap that had opened between us, but I didn't know how. The weight of my secrets pressed down on me, and I felt trapped.

"It's complicated," I finally said, my eyes avoiding his piercing gaze.

"Goodnight Julianna." His voice held no emotion as he stepped inside and closed the door, leaving me standing alone under the porch light, my heart heavy with regret and longing.

———

Morning came too early.

I'd tossed and turned the entire night, not happy one bit with how our evening had turned out. As my feet hit the floor, I resolved to make this right.

I sat next to Chase in our favorite booth at *Ringo's Diner*. We didn't talk about last night. Then again, neither of us really tried. We were meeting Sam, and hopefully after spending time with me in a neutral atmosphere, Chase would be over himself and we could have a conversation.

"Juli! Chase! Good morning." Sam smiled wide as he slid into the booth across from us.

"Can I get you guys something to drink?" Scott Iverson shook a piece of his shaggy blond hair out of his eyes as he handed us menus.

"Coffee all around?" I asked the men, to which they nodded and opened their menus.

"Great, I'll be right back with those."

"How long are you here again?" Chase asked Sam.

"Just the summer. I'm helping my father through the fair, then I will work with my future brother-in-law in the restaurant."

"Future?" I asked and thanked Scott when he delivered our coffee.

"My sister Trini is getting married, and our father wants Ravi to work with him in the family business."

"That's nice." I smiled, hoping to brighten the underlying mood vibrating from Chase.

"We shall see, Juli. You do not know my father." Sam chuckled. "I worry there may not be a wedding." He shrugged and sipped his coffee.

"I take it you don't like the guy?" Chase raised the steaming cup to his lips.

"Oh, we all like him very much. The question is, can he work with Baba."

Our laughter broke up as Rita approached with a beverage carrier, holding two large coffees and a bag of breakfast to go that smelled like heaven.

"Hi, I'm sorry to interrupt," she said and smiled politely at Sam. "Have either of you seen Paul?" Chase and I both shook our heads. "Of course, we got into a very heated discussion at the fair last night after David left."

Chase cleared his throat at the mention of David, then buried his face in the menu.

"Is everything okay? Were you able to talk it out?" I asked, taking a sip of coffee and a sideward glance toward Chase, who remained unfazed.

"For the most part. He told me he was going back to the gym tent to get his insulin because he was going to need it by the time he got home. When he checked in with me later, he told me not to worry but he still needed some space to digest everything. At that point he was going to grab the couch in Ivan's hotel room. Must be he's still there." She shrugged. "And girl … you and I are going to have to talk."

At that comment, Chase snapped his head up and I felt the intensity of his gaze without having to look at him. Oh boy, making things right was going to cost me more than a cup of coffee and breakfast. It was my turn to clear my throat and swallow what little pride I had left.

"I agree."

"Why don't you stop by the fair later and I'll show you the progress I've made on your project. It's amazing what I can do with dedicated time. And people love my creations!" Rita glowed with happiness.

"I can't wait. I'll catch up with you later."

"Okay, bye." Rita smiled at us and left the diner.

"Who was that vision of beauty?" Sam questioned as he followed Rita's exit until he couldn't twist any further in his seat. He righted himself and leaned his forearms on the table. "No, seriously guys, I think I'm in love."

"Easy killer," Chase leaned back, and it was nice to see a genuine smile on his face again. "She's spoken for."

"Then I guess now I'm going to have to order the stuffed French toast and what is it you say? Eat my feelings?"

"You'd better hold off on ordering." Gary appeared next to our table, and I almost jumped out of my seat. "Didn't mean to scare you, Juli."

"Why, what's going on?" Chase straightened his spine, immediately on alert and ready to take action.

"We have a situation."

"Don't even tell me it has something to do with the Ross

brothers," Chase growled and swiped a hand down his face in frustration. "They are the last thing I need right now."

"No, they are still sleeping it off."

"Everything okay with Liam? Sorry I haven't had much time to spend with him. I appreciate you stepping up with the rookie."

"Marty stayed overnight so Liam could go home and relieve him at noon."

"Then what is it?" Chase narrowed his eyes, and my worry meter flickered.

"Can I ... speak with you in private?"

Chase rose from the booth and followed Gary toward the door. I watched their postures, so rigid, hands on hips as they leaned forward, speaking things they didn't want anyone else to hear. When he returned to our table, it was to drain the coffee from his cup.

"Sorry, gotta go."

"What's going on?" I asked, ready to follow.

"They found a body at the fairgrounds."

Five

"Is that ..." I covered my mouth and turned my head away.

"Paul Rivera." Chase confirmed, shaking his head in dismay. "Do we know what happened?" He directed his question to Gary.

"Not yet. There's no visible wound that I could see. With all those bruises, it's hard to tell if he got into another scuffle, or fell into the weight bench and equipment here in the tent."

"Oh, my gosh ... Rita." My heart sank as I realized Rita had no clue what had happened. Chase and Gary shifted their focus to me, waiting for my reaction. "She thinks he's still at Ivan's hotel." My eyes drifted to Paul's lifeless body, and I felt an overwhelming sense of sorrow for my friend. "I need to be there for her."

"Not so fast." Chase stopped my forward motion. "Until we have all the facts, I don't want you saying anything. If anyone is going to tell her, it's got to be me or Gary."

"Right." I shook my head, reality not totally sinking in.

"Did you call Rip?" Chase said while keeping an eye on me.

Gary crouched near a rack of dumbbells and replied, "When I was on my way to find you."

"Who's Rip?" I questioned.

"The coroner," Gary and Chase said in unison, their faces still troubled in thought.

"That's either a horrible choice, or uncanny coincidence." I rubbed the chills off my arms as I glanced around the tent, looking for a potential clue. Everything seemed in order.

"His real name is Conrad Ripton." Gary used his pen to push a wrinkled piece of material into an evidence bag. "And he really likes the nickname."

"I take it this is all your doing?" I pointed at Chase.

"No. He was given the name by some co-workers." He stepped away to walk the perimeter of the tent.

"Like I said, he really likes it," Gary added. "He should be here any minute."

"Hey, mister, you can't go in there!" someone yelled.

"Meanwhile, Rita is home alone," I said, my ears tuning into a commotion outside the tent.

I spun around, my heart pounding in my chest, only to be met with the sight of my stone-cold-serious ex, David. He was sipping a cup of coffee, his gaze scanning the crime scene with an air of authority, as if he had every right to be there. The memories of our past together came rushing back, unbidden and unwelcome, clouding my thoughts. His mere presence a stark reminder of old wounds that had never quite healed.

"She's fine, darling. I just left her." The all too familiar voice cooed. *Was I ever going to be rid of him?*

I clenched my fists, trying to steady my racing emotions, knowing I had to stay focused on the task at hand. I rushed to stand in front of him, my voice low, "What are you doing here?"

"Exactly what I would like to know." Slowly I turned, eyes wide and desperately trying to mask the turmoil churning inside. The low vibrato of Chase's voice sent shivers down my spine, freezing me in place as my breath caught in my throat. "You've got some nerve crossing that line."

David shrugged. "Hmm ... Too bad about Paul," he stated as he casually strolled around us to stand over Paul's body.

"I'm going to have to ask you to leave. This is a crime scene." Chase reached toward David, but I cut him off.

"I got this. David, let's go."

"She's better off without the musclehead anyway. I've spent most of this morning trying to convince her."

"Are you serious?" I latched on to David's elbow and steered him away from the scene. "Stay out of her relationship. And mine, too," I ground out as he and Chase exchanged a fierce, unyielding glare, filled with intensity and unspoken challenges.

"I've done nothing wrong, Julianna. I called her to see if she was okay. I didn't trust that man in her life. She deserves better and she needed to know that."

"You don't even know Paul. You have no reason to be giving her any kind of advice."

"Let's just say he and I had a little chat."

"You spoke to him? After the little fist fight you two had?" My mind was spinning, and I hoped Chase or Gary weren't listening. This did not look good.

"You know I'm not one to mince words." He shot me a sly grin. "Or kiss and tell."

"Stop." I chanced a quick glance at Chase whose vision was laser focused on me.

"Settle down, darling. I know you and I have some unfinished business, but I needed to stop Rita from making a mistake."

"Like the one she made with you? The one I *almost* made with you?" I straightened my spine and locked my eyes on his. He didn't even flinch. "See, you won't even try to deny it."

"I've had a lot of time to think about things since your disappearing act. My infatuation with you was my downfall. I should have left the romance out of it, and for that I'm sorry." He hitched a shoulder, dismissing what we'd had so easily. "But Rita, we had some memorable moments together. A marriage we were both into until I messed up by focusing too much on business."

"Like you were doing with me? That kind of business?" The words tumbled out and I couldn't take them back. What happened back in Boston had been underhanded and shady. "You know I figured it out, right? I told you everything, and I was right."

"You were wrong."

"No." I shook my head. "I saw it all with my own eyes. I know what you were doing. You were letting it happen, and now I think you were setting me up to take the fall. Only I beat you to it."

"Beat him to what?" Chase joined our conversation, and I couldn't be more thankful for his presence, though the tension in the air thickened.

"Leaving my business," David added, his tone dripping with disdain, "which is none of yours."

"We'll see about that." Chase narrowed his eyes, his voice low and dangerous. "And that's all? I've gotta tell you, it sounded like a lot more."

I stayed silent, my mind racing with questions. What kind of game was David playing? And what was Rita's part in it? The cup he held came from *Ringo's*, there was no denying the signature barber pole striped Styrofoam, and he'd basically confirmed he'd been talking to her. But why?

"I assure you, Sheriff, there's nothing more," David said, his voice steady but his eyes betraying a flicker of uncertainty.

"And I assure *you*, Mr. von Hoffster, there is," Chase countered, his gaze unwavering.

Both David and I stared at Chase in wonder, the tension crackling between us like a live wire.

"What could that possibly be?" David scoffed, though his bravado seemed forced.

"That you've returned to the scene of the crime. From the information my team just gathered, this looks like a crime of passion, Chase stated in a cold and accusatory tone.

"You think I killed the musclehead?" David's hearty laughter cut through the somber air, but there was a nervous edge to it. "You couldn't be farther from the truth."

"Tell me, where were you between your fight with the victim last night and this morning? And why is it you have a tear in your shirt that happens to match this piece of material my Deputy found just moments before you arrived?" Chase's voice was relentless, each word a hammering blow.

"Chase!" I couldn't believe what I was hearing. Chase obviously didn't hear me, he was too busy antagonizing David.

"After everything I just overheard, you not only have motive, but you were the last person seen physically fighting with the man, over Rita Davis no less. The same woman you are still married to, and who you've spent the morning with, judging by that cup from the diner," Chase continued, his eyes never leaving David's.

"Highly observant, Sherrif. But you're still wrong. It's not a crime to buy coffee from the local diner, and I did not kill the man. I'm not saying another word without my lawyer," David said, his voice now tinged with defiance.

"Have it your way. Gary, take Mr. von Hoffster to the station as a person of interest until his lawyer shows up. Liam can release the Ross brothers. We've got bigger fish to fry, and I want that piece of material analyzed, stat!"

I stared in shock as Gary cuffed David and led him away from the scene. This was all happening so fast. I hadn't even had time to process David still being married to Rita when he proposed, now he was being taken to jail.

"What is going on?" I demanded, my voice breaking as I stared Chase down.

"Why don't you tell me." He crossed his arms, creating an imposing stance in front of me.

"You're seriously arresting him?"

"Shouldn't I?" He arched a brow, a hint of challenge to his tone.

"No. No you shouldn't." I stepped closer, boldly uncrossing his arms. "David didn't do this. He didn't kill Paul."

"Right now, he's the number one suspect, unless you know something different."

"I ..." My voice faltered, the weight of the situation crushing my chest.

"Yes?"

"I know for certain David did not kill Paul Rivera."

"Explain."

"I can't."

"Can't, or won't?"

"What?" I stammered, catching a mix of emotions swirling like a tornado in his deep green eyes. Swallowing hard, I felt the ache in my chest over the revealing truth that no matter what he'd said the other night, he still didn't believe in me. "I can't believe you." I didn't try to hide the hurt I felt, and his countenance didn't change.

"Tell me why I should believe you."

"Because it's me. Me and you, we have this ... this *thing*!" I flailed my arms in the air. "Don't do this to us again. I'm asking you to believe me, believe *in me*."

"How?" It was his turn to raise his arms, and his voice. "Juli, I have given you every opportunity, but you never take it. You can't expect me to believe in you when you won't trust me enough to tell me the truth."

"Chase, this is different."

"No, Juli. This is you, it's what you do."

The truth hit my own ears hard, and I felt the sting of tears. He had to see I was trying. "Not anymore. Not since I've come home."

"You can't even tell me why you're sticking up for him. He obviously hurt you, but you refuse to tell me why or let me in to whatever it was that happened in Boston. I bet that has something to do with your ex-whatever-he-is showing up in *my* town. I want answers, Julianna. If you're not giving them to me, then I'll find them on my own."

"David may be a jerk and a royal pain, but he's not a killer."

"Says the woman with her own suitcase of secrets. Stay out of this case, Julianna, or you'll be sharing a cell with the suspect. Is that understood?"

All I could do was nod.

"Good. Get to your store, it's business as usual. Do not contact Rita. I'm going to finish up with Rip, pick up Gary and we'll head over to see her." Chase started walking away, then turned with a final warning. "Don't test me on this. Stay away from this case."

While I hated what was happening between us, I also knew I happened to be the only other person besides Rita who knew David best. David might be a pot-stirrer, but he wasn't a murderer. Chase knew I'd never stay away, especially now.

I had more to prove than just whodunnit.

Six

"Rita I'm so sorry about Paul," I said that night, once Gary gave me the okay to see her. I'd brought a bottle of red wine to her house, but neither one of us had taken a sip.

"I just don't understand how this happened." She curled her knees tighter beneath her, sinking deeper into the cranberry-colored fabric of her sofa. With a stretch, she reached for another tissue from the end table. "Why would anyone want to kill Paul?"

"I don't know. You can bet Chase will find the answers you need." It didn't matter what was going on between us now. I knew how seriously he took his job and how much he loved this town. In my short time back, New Hope had grown on me in ways I never imagined.

"I hope so, Juli. We had made such plans and now ... they are all gone." Rita buried her face into a pillow and sobbed. "Paul was my soul mate."

I cleared my throat, feeling uncomfortable with the thoughts going through my head. Gary told me he and Chase talked with Rita. He didn't say they'd questioned her, but rather consoled her. Rita and I had one common bond. Someone who had inserted himself in New Hope for reasons I still didn't know for certain. I had to ask the question before Chase did.

"About David ..." I spoke softly, but the words carried weight. Rita's head snapped up from the pillow, her eyes bloodshot.

"I know how this looks, Juli, but it's not what you think."

"When you picked up your order at *Ringo's*, that was for you and David wasn't it?"

"Yes." She sniffed. "We had things to iron out."

"The divorce."

"And other things."

"It seems like the divorce would be the most important. Once it was officially final, you would be free to make any plans with Paul that you wanted."

"David wants me back," Rita blurted out, while keeping her eyes on the cranberry and gold pillow still in her lap.

"What?" The vision of Rita reaching for the glass of wine swam before my eyes, and I still hadn't had a drop. "Why?"

"He admitted he never should have let me go."

"And what about *me*?" Again, I couldn't believe I'd spoken out loud. I didn't care what David thought of me, not anymore. But in some weird way, I wanted closure. "Why would he lead me on?" Only I knew the answer to that question.

"He told me he was so infatuated with your free spirit and your beauty. He genuinely wanted to marry you. He saw a future with you by his side. He said you are brilliant in the art world and his gallery wasn't the same after you left."

"Yeah, I bet."

"He had time to think about his behavior. With you, with me, with his business." She paused to sip more wine. "He came here to find you, you know."

"Me?" Of course he did. He wanted the painting back. "I made myself very clear when I left. There was no misinterpreting my statement."

"He said that, too. He came here to apologize, thinking he could convince you to return to Boston for the sake of the gallery."

"Then why didn't he?"

"Because he found me here, too." She swiped at her eyes.

"Wait a minute. Are you seriously thinking about getting back with David? Is that why you and Paul were fighting?"

"No!" She sat up straight. "I mean, not right away. Paul and I argued at the fairgrounds once everyone went their own way. I told him I was going home, but he said he needed to get things ready for today and the body building competition tomorrow afternoon."

"But you said he didn't stay here."

"No. I called him as it got later, and he said he was still angry over the whole David thing and how I never told him I had been married before. He was hurt, and I understood that. He said he was going to stay with Ivan at his hotel and that he needed some space." Rita paused, and I saw love and sadness in her eyes. "We told each other I love you. We knew we'd be okay. We had to get over this bump in the road."

Boy, did I know about bumps. Right now, I felt like Chase and I were sinking deep into a pothole. We hadn't even come close to saying the "L" word. I figured it was implied to a certain degree.

"Then somebody killed him," Rita said on a shaky breath. "I can't for the life of me figure out who, or why."

"Which leads us back to David. If he still loved you and wanted you back, could he have gotten angry enough with Paul to fight him again?" My gut didn't believe that it was possible. For that matter, what was Rita's alibi? Did she decide she still loved David after finding out they were still married? She could have argued with Paul and killed him in a crime of passion and was now covering her tracks. I didn't know what to believe or who to trust anymore.

"David called me to tell me he'd run into Paul leaving the fairgrounds. David told Paul he loved me and wasn't giving up without a fight."

"He does like to have things his own way," I mused, and we both laughed a little bit uncomfortably before Rita's eyes grew dark and serious.

"Paul wanted to fight again. But David said no, it should be up to me to decide who I wanted to spend the rest of my life with."

"Fair, I guess."

"I had another conversation with Paul once he got to Ivan's hotel. He and Ivan were having a planning session. I guess there was a problem with someone they were going to choose to be the manager at the new location."

"Who was that?"

"I don't know. Paul never told me. We made plans to meet up once we got to our tents today."

"And David?"

"I told him I'm in love with and marrying Paul."

"Ouch, how did he take it?"

"Okay, I guess." She shrugged. "He's the one who suggested breakfast so we could continue our discussion."

I finally reached for my glass. "Don't you think David's getting the wrong idea?"

Rita shook her head. "He knows where we stand right now." Then she added sadly, "Especially now."

"Which is?" The shocked stare she pinned on me stung a little. The more she talked the more this sounded like a twisted love triangle, except Paul was dead. And David seemed guilty enough without a shadow of doubt.

"There is no future." She exhaled her frustration. "There wasn't before Paul was murdered, and there sure isn't now."

"I'm sorry, I didn't mean anything." I felt horrible for second guessing her, but something felt off.

She shook her head. "I'm sure you didn't. You don't know what it feels like to be so close to having everything you've ever dreamed of only to turn around and find it gone right out from under you."

Those were the words that haunted me when I returned home and crawled into bed for another fitful sleep over one handsome lawman and a past returning to haunt me with what appeared to be a vengeance.

———

I WALKED INTO CHASE'S OFFICE WITHOUT KNOCKING. His space was a blend of rustic charm and no-nonsense functionality. An imposing wooden desk dominated the room, its surface meticulously organized with case files and a vintage lamp casting a warm glow. His worn leather chair hinted at long hours spent behind the desk, while framed commendations and photographs tracked his career and dedication to the community. The scent of leather and aged paper filled the room, mingling with the faint aroma of brewed coffee, creating an atmosphere that was both inviting and authoritative.

I closed the door behind me, and presented the tray of blueberry, raspberry and strawberry goodies on the corner of his desk. He glanced up from a file he'd been reading, closed it and set it precisely on top of what I assumed to be his TBR pile.

"What's this, a peace offering or a bribe?" He narrowed his eyes.

"Neither." I avoided his gaze, hating to admit what came next. "I couldn't sleep."

"That makes two of us, Scarlett." His tone was rough and strained.

I released my captive breath and held his stare. The circles under his eyes were evident, as well as the slight shadow to his beard, leading me to believe he didn't have time to shave. He rose from his desk and reached a hand toward my hair.

"You have flour--"

"Everywhere, I know." I grinned, and I saw the corner of his mouth twitch. "You should see my kitchen. I wanted to stop by before you got too busy."

"Never too busy for you, you know that." He still held the auburn strand between his fingers, lifting it so his thumb could brush telltale flour off my cheek. The vibe between us still contained our magic and I felt, like Rita had with Paul, that we would be okay. It was only a bump in the road.

"I thought maybe we—" My sentence was cut off by Deputy Maxwell who strolled in carrying two cups of steaming coffee.

"Chase, I've got some information on—" He stopped short. "Oh, hey, Juli. Surprised to see you here. Did you bring us snacks?" He licked his lips once he spotted the tray, handing a cup in Chase's direction.

"They are mini vegan cheesecakes," I announced proudly. "My own recipe."

"Vegan?" Chase dropped the strand of hair so he could take the cup from Gary. "You're trying to kill me, aren't you?" he said, returning to his desk.

"They smell fantastic," Gary said, smiling wide.

"Don't encourage her." Chase's gaze returned to the report he'd been reading.

"Don't be such a skeptic." I raised my chin a notch. "I guarantee you'll love these."

"Maybe." He fought not to grin. "What I don't love is a town full of people and a murder. I'm going to have to call in support to make sure people aren't leaving town, and no new people are coming in."

"You mean we're all in lockdown?" I reached across the desk, slipped the coffee cup from his hand and took a sip. "Yuck! How can you drink it like that?" I grimaced, holding the cup away from my lips. How could I forget he drank his coffee black.

"No baby additives." He smoothly took possession of the cup

and held it up in salute before taking another sip. "And yes, a lockdown."

"We need to make sure David's story sticks." Gary picked up a blueberry cheesecake, and I watched his eyes roll back in complete satisfaction after he took a bite. "Mmm ... Juli, these are fantastic." He popped the rest in his mouth and proceeded to grab the other flavors. "Chase, you've got to try one, man. Amazing!"

"Maybe later. We have work to do." He eyed my creations cautiously, took a strawberry one and set it on his desk. "Was there anything else?" He asked me.

"Well, now that you mention David's story, I have some news after being with Rita for a while last night."

"I know, she called me after you left. Apparently, she thinks we're working the case together. Any thought as to how she got that idea?"

"First off, we were partners on the Seaver case."

"No, we weren't."

"Okay, so I was a consultant. Whatever. The point is, we made a great team." I held up a hand to stop his next remark. "Regardless of what you want to say, I basically told Rita you love this town, and you will find out who killed Paul."

"Considering we have our number one suspect already in custody, all we need now is to crack him open. Find out what he knows and why he did it." Chase leaned back in his chair.

"He doesn't have an alibi, and the motive of jealous ex-lover seems to be fitting for now," Gary added, taking a sip of his coffee. "We just need to find the murder weapon and make sure he's not working with anyone else, where other people could be in danger."

"From David?" I laughed. "You guys are way off base. That's why I'm here."

"Do you know something?" Chase rose from his chair, the lightness he'd had a moment ago turning rigid.

"Makes sense," Gary interrupted. "She does have a history with the guy."

"You don't have to remind me," Chase ground out.

"Listen, David von Hoffster is not a killer." I crossed my arms at their disbelieving stares.

"You saw the same taunting and fight I did, right?"

"Of course, but that's David. He likes to make himself look good. He's all about appearances. That man could not commit murder." A syndicated crime, maybe, but not stone-cold murder.

"You keep saying that, but where's my proof?" Chase held out his hand.

"My word. And where's your proof that he committed the crime?"

"Juli. I need more than that and you know it. Doesn't Paul deserve justice? Doesn't Rita deserve the truth?"

I stood quietly, wanting to explain what David's motivation was. Even though it incriminated him even more, he would never have taken someone else's life. Knowing what Paul meant to Rita and that David still loved her was all the proof I needed. He would never have hurt Rita like this. He wanted a fair fight.

And I had no idea how to convince Chase of any of it.

"Yes, Sheriff-Goody. But I have a proposition." I took a cleansing breath, channeling every bit of my wonderful mother I could. This would be tricky, but I was counting on my lawman's compassionate nature to agree with me. "Remember that time you had me come and stay with you to make sure nothing happened after my house was broken into and that horrible voodoo doll appeared?"

"That was for your own safety." He squinted as he studied me. "Where are you going with this because if it's where I'm thinking, it's a big fat no."

"But you haven't even heard my idea." My voice climbed several octaves as frustration took over. *Sorry, Mom.*

"Not gonna happen."

"Chase, David will talk to me. I can get information firsthand."

"No." He pursed his lips and firmly shook his head.

"Gary, a little help here?" I turned my focus on the adorable deputy.

"Sorry, Juli, I'll gladly referee, but I'm not getting in the middle of this one."

"Smart man," Chase nodded in his partner's direction.

"You two are unbelievable. Give me twenty-four hours," I pleaded.

"To do what exactly?" Chase twirled a pencil between his fingers.

"You know, kind of like house arrest? Only it's my house, he's me and I'm you."

"Juli ..." The warning in his voice didn't stop me. I was on a mission.

"Don't you Juli me. Doesn't David deserve justice, too, Sheriff?" I paused when my words garnered more attention.

"We're waiting on his attorney."

"Good, then naturally he needs a friend more than ever, Chase. And that's me."

"Is there something more you need to tell me?" Those green eyes stared deep into my soul.

Oh, there was a long list of things I needed to tell him, but David being a suspect right now moved to the top. I chewed the inside of my cheek as I mentally scanned my list to see if there was something I could give him right now that might sway his decision.

"No, nothing at all. You need to believe me."

"Oh, we're having this discussion again. Now is not the time, Julianna."

"Then let me take him home." Oof, wrong choice of words, judging by the reddened face of my favorite lawman. "Not that way! To talk."

"Considering your prior fiancée status, leaving him to return to New Hope and now he randomly shows up, potentially killing someone ... the answer is still no." He rose from his chair and said, "I don't trust him."

"Chase!" I stormed after him as he left his office.

"You can talk to him through the bars. Now if you'll excuse me, I've got a job to do." He dipped his head before donning his hat and leaving the station.

I glanced at the cell where David sat looking sad ... or bored, I couldn't tell. I was on my own with this one. It wasn't going to be easy because I knew why he came to town, and I was not about to let the painting go. I was owed that money, and then some. The painting more than made up for my salary and the suffering I had endured. I needed David cleared and back in Boston where he belonged. If Eddie was here, then trouble wouldn't be far behind.

Which meant Scallywag had been right.

Seven

David lay flat on the cot with forearms crossed over his eyes. The drama was just too much with this man sometimes. "Julianna, I want to thank you for trying to get me out of this damp, dismal prison cell. I don't belong here."

"I know you don't. I'm going to get you out, don't worry."

"You're serious?" He sat up and eyed me warily. "You'd do that for me? I thought you hated me after—"

"Hate is a strong word. Let's say I was extremely angry with you." I leaned my forehead against the cool iron bars of his cell. "I don't want to get into that right now. We have more important things to talk about."

I wasn't sure how long Chase and Gary would be out, but I had questions for David that I didn't need either one of them to hear right now. Once I pieced everything together then I would fill them both in.

"I get why you came into town, but why is Eddie here? You know he's not my favorite person."

"Eddie? Darling, what are you talking about?" David approached the bars and put his hands over mine. "I have no idea where Eddie is. He literally disappeared about the same time as you."

I pulled my hands away and crossed my arms. "What? That can't be. I swear I saw him at the fairgrounds last night." Well, his hat anyway. An eerie chill swept across my skin. Eddie was bad news. "I was at the top of the Ferris wheel, so maybe I was mistaken."

"This is not Eddie's scene."

"No, it's not, but he has a way of making you do things out of character for you. I thought maybe he followed you."

"I make my own decisions. You know that from working with me, among other things."

"David, we're not talking about us. Not now, not ever again." I wasn't just clearing his name for his sake. I needed to clear my past.

"Ah, you still have feelings for Sheriff Hargrave. *Your* ex." He whistled low and soft. "Seems like once again we have something in common."

"Maybe." I shook my head to clear the distraction he caused. "Why don't you tell me about your conversation with Rita. I need to know everything, David, if I'm going to help you. I need to make sure that both of your stories stick because right now, it's not looking good."

"You talked to Rita? How is she? What did she tell you?"

"She said she told you she loved Paul and was going to marry him. Is that right?"

"Yes."

"And what did you do? Did you fight him again?"

"No, but he wanted to. I simply told him I was prepared to fight for her. He was still mad over our divorce never being finalized. He took a couple more swings at me, but I told him we needed to let Rita decide."

"She chose Paul," I said firmly, hoping to ground him in the reality of his situation.

"I know. All I told her was to think about what we shared for almost five years."

"And then what?"

"She didn't tell you?" He shot me a sideward glance, and I shook my head. "She agreed to take some time, especially since she felt like the musclehead was overreacting. That was all I needed."

"Is that why you met her for coffee?"

"I what?" He seemed genuinely confused.

"Coffee. She went to *Ringo's* and got you both breakfast so you could discuss the situation?"

"Oh right, right. Sorry. This hellhole has me all out of sorts, and my lawyer is taking forever to get here."

"Trust me, I know how you feel." I thought of my own jail time which had been cut short thanks to Major and Scallywag. "Give me some time with Chase. I'm pretty sure I can convince him to let me keep an eye on you."

"I've got nothing but time, darling." David reached through the bars and tweaked my nose. "I can't blame him, you know. I wouldn't trust me with you, either."

I ignored his comment. "Well, he can trust me, and so can you. You and I are over. I care about you as a friend only and I will do what I can to help you." I stepped back from the cell. "Keep thinking of anything you might have seen out of the ordinary when you went to talk to Paul. Descriptions of other people hanging around, or anything at all that seems suspicious."

"I'll try but I was so focused on telling that muscle bound jerk where he could go. I almost bumped into some sweet little thing as I was leaving his tent."

"What did she look like?" I raced to grab a scrap of paper and a pen off Gary's desk.

"I really wasn't paying attention."

"Think, David! This could be very important."

"I'm not sure. It was getting dark, there were other people milling around."

"It's a county fair, what did you expect." I paused to take him in, sitting on the cot as if he were at summer camp not really concerned about which activity he was going to sign up for. Unbelievable. "You do understand the severity of what's happening, right? You're the number one suspect in a murder investigation."

"I know."

"Then please take this seriously. Any detail, no matter how minor it might seem to you could be the break in your case and clear your name."

"I know how the law works, Julianna. I think you should go. This has been a stressful day, and I doubt your sheriff and his deputies will even feed me. These accommodations are simply deplorable."

"Why am I even bothering with you?" I spun around to leave and then whipped back to his cell. "Oh wait, I know why. Because you, David von Hoffster, need to return to Boston immediately so my life can return to normal."

"I thought you were going to help me?" He hit me with the saddest puppy dog eyes I'd ever seen.

"I am," I said on an exasperated sigh. "I need you to work with me on this or I will let the good sheriff take over and he's ready to ship you off right now."

"I promise, I will cooperate." He nodded and I believed him, at least for now.

"Good. I have to go but I will check in with you later. I'll bring some snacks from my café, just in case they forget to feed you." I paused, enjoying the shock on his face a little too much. "Behave," I warned and walked out. My worry meter hummed once more. Something told me David was keeping something important from me.

Now I knew how Chase felt.

———

I LEFT THE JAIL FEELING HOPEFUL AND READY TO START my own investigations. The young woman who visited Paul after David left added a new twist. Did they fight? Rita never mentioned Paul had an ex-girlfriend. Then again, Rita never told Paul she had an ex-husband. That could be a relevant coincidence.

When I reached *The Butler's Pantry*, the door pushed open before my key was fully inserted into the lock. After Pete Seaver's murder was solved, I'd made sure to have the old locks replaced. I eased the door open all the way, peeking inside before going further.

Everything was quiet.

I sighed with relief and closed the door, welcoming the sound of my wooden chimes. I was sure I locked up yesterday. Andie Evans, my full-time barista, had a key to the café door in the back. I always opened that earlier than the pantry side. Maybe she came in to grab stock for our booth at the fair and had gone out the front door? I decided to keep the café closed and take all the business to the fair, leaving me alone on *The Butler's Pantry* side to keep up with orders in the kitchen and restock treats and samples for the fair. Before going into the kitchen, I headed for the café door, to make sure it hadn't been left open, too.

"Simon!" I gasped when I saw the tall man looking into my antique ice chest, one of the statement pieces from Mom that I loved. "What are you doing here?" I walked past him toward the door, and sure enough it was locked.

"I'm here for our appointment." He held up his camera by the strap around his neck. "Your door was unlocked, so I thought you were here. I've only been here about five minutes. Hope you don't mind, I couldn't help admiring some of your antiques while I waited for you."

"We had an appointment?" I questioned, pulling up the calendar on my phone. The man still had his sunglasses on. The unsettled feeling returned to my gut.

"We talked about me doing a shoot of *Petite Four Paws* and *The Butler's Pantry*. You have some fantastic lighting in this place."

"I'm so sorry, I don't remember, and I don't even have it on my calendar." I scrolled again for good measure. "I'm so busy with back orders from my grand opening and keeping up with the fair, I really can't do anything until next week when it's over."

"No worries, Juli. You can always give me a call when you're ready. I have some friends who would gladly post my photos and articles. It will be great publicity for you."

"Thanks, Simon. I appreciate it. New Hope is so small, sometimes I wonder how people will find out about me. Every bit of advertising helps."

"No problem at all." He paused and bent to pick something up off the floor. "By the way, I fed your kitten."

"My—" I sighed in exasperation when Simon cradled Steve between his hands. "Tess."

"That's a cute name for a kitten, but I'm pretty sure it's a boy." He turned the cat's tummy toward himself for a parts check. "Yup, Tess is a boy."

I laughed, shaking my head and taking custody of the sleek, black feline. "Yes, his name is Steve. Tess McDermot keeps sneaking in here and hiding him in all sorts of places for me to find. What am I going to do with you?" I nuzzled his little pink nose against mine and his tiny motor revved on high.

"He obviously likes you." Simon reached to pet him. "Why don't you keep him?"

I stood quiet for a moment, enjoying the soothing purr of my companion. "I'm not ready to be a cat-mom. I have a crazy parrot in the house next door, a needy sheepdog on the other side of my house, and I babysit both animals at random times. With all the work I'm doing to get my business up and running, I don't think it would be fair for him to be left alone all day."

"He seems to do fine here. It is a pet café after all. He should stay here, then you wouldn't have to worry."

"Are you working for Tess?" I chided and set Steve on the floor where he proceeded to stretch his white mittened paws in a pool of sunshine.

"Not at all."

"Then why don't you adopt him. Better yet," I paused as I recognized my growing affection for Steve, "I'm sure Tess would gladly give you Fluffy or Cotton. Take one home to your wife and kids."

"Ahhh, that's okay." He held up both palms as if in surrender. "My wife is highly allergic to animals."

"Aw, that's too bad. The brothers are adorable, too." I smiled as Steve's tail curled and straightened as if in agreement.

"Hey, listen, reach out when you're ready for the shoot. My house has had some delays with the contractors so I'm still at The Sunflower Inn."

"I'm sure Misty loves having you."

"Misty does, but I'm not sure about my waistline." Simon patted his stomach. "I think I've gained ten pounds."

"I always see you out walking. I'm sure you're fine." I stared at his face, wishing I could see his eyes. He was so hard to read. "Besides, Misty uses all natural ingredients. You're probably eating healthier than you've ever been while traveling."

"If you say so." Simon walked toward the front door, and I noticed how he took everything in.

My eyes followed his around the space I had redesigned myself, proud of the changes in what had been my mother's antique store. I think I was most proud of putting down roots and finally admitting my home had always been here. Simon's voice pulled me from my thoughts.

"Too bad about that David fellow, huh? I hear you know him?"

"Yes, for a few years when I was in Boston."

"Do you think he did it? He shows up in town and then Paul Rivera is dead? Seems suspicious to me."

"The sheriff is working on it. Right now, David is the only suspect. I'm sure the sheriff's investigation will turn up others. He's very good at what he does."

"Of course. He's very respected here. I'm sure he's feeling the pressure, though, after collaborating with the FBI on the Seaver murder."

"What? Oh, right," I said trying to stay focused. I should have known the rumor mill would have spread about me and David and Rita. No wonder Chase was putting some distance between us. "He's not in this for the recognition." I found myself defending him.

"Well, I hope it all works out for you and Rita." Simon opened the door and turned to face me. "Has the sheriff thought about questioning Ms. Davis? I'm sure she's upset and all, since they were engaged, but I did see her with that David guy the other night in the parking lot when I drove by *Pepper's Motel*. Given her past with the man, I think she would be a person of interest." Simon nodded and walked out. I stared at the door for a good five minutes as what he said sank in.

Rita never mentioned meeting David at *Pepper's*. Maybe it was time I had a conversation with my favorite lawman. If we put our heads together, we might be able to get closer to finding the real killer.

Because I still believed in David's innocence. No matter how strange that sounded.

Eight

Fifteen frantic minutes later, Chase arrived at my shop. I hadn't stopped shaking since discovering another voodoo doll sitting inside one of my bamboo mixing bowls. This time there was a typed note pinned to its chest.

"I'm watching you." Chase repeated the message, giving it more weight and causing another round of chills across my body. "I thought these were done?"

"Me, too. I have only ever had the one back in my kitchen before we solved Pete's murder." I remembered walking through my ransacked house until I saw the doll tied to a wooden spoon and a paring knife stuck through it. "This time, everything is the way I left it. They weren't searching for anything. Why would someone leave this in my shop? Pete's murder is solved, everything has been fine."

"Maybe it doesn't have anything to do with Pete's murder." Chase draped his arm across my shoulders and pulled me close.

"Do you think it has to do with Paul's murder?" I stepped back. "Why me?"

"Tell me what happened when you got here." Chase went into investigation mode, notebook and all. His presence calmed my nerves, and I had no problem recapping when I walked into the shop, and being startled by Simon Banks.

"I guess I didn't write down our appointment. He did say the door was already open when he got here, which is why he came in. When he realized I wasn't here, he decided to stick around until I returned."

"Interesting."

"Wait a minute, do you think Simon did this?" The thought had occurred to me the moment I found the doll, but I didn't want to believe it. "Why? I don't know him."

"None of us know him. He comes and goes, yet continues to stay at the *Sunflower Inn*, basically keeps to himself other than conversations with Misty Shepard."

"He mentioned his family to me. He discovered Steve before I got here." I pointed toward the sleeping kitten, still sprawled on the floor, and shrugged. "Maybe Tess somehow got in to drop off Steve? Regardless, I mentioned to Simon that he should take the kitten home to his family."

"What did he say to that?"

"His wife is very allergic to cats. We talked a little more and then he left and told me to reach out once the fair is over so he can take some pictures and write an article about *The Butler's Pantry*. He knows people who would easily repost and spread the word."

"That's great, but it's not helping us figure out who is still threatening you," Chase said, his tone steady and authoritative, a frown deepening the lines on his face.

"Why did you have to use that word?" I asked, my voice faltering.

"How else would you think to describe first the paring knife, and now an actual message that you are being watched?" he replied, his eyes sharp and unyielding.

"Secret admirer?" I tilted my head, attempting to be coy, a small smile playing at the corners of my lips.

"Not funny, Scarlett." His voice was firm, his expression unamused.

"It's either that or have another meltdown, and I'd rather not. I have too much on my mind and too much to do."

"I take it you mean David von Hoffster?" Chase placed the palms of his hands on the black and white quartz island where I prepared all my organic recipes. He waited patiently while I mentally ran through my files on David and what I was ready to own up to. "Listen," he continued when I didn't speak up. "I understand your need to defend him and be there for him."

"You do?" It was my turn to be shocked.

"Believe it or not, April helped me see the light."

"April? You went to her for help?" How could he do that? I couldn't mask the frustration on my face.

"Don't get mad. I ran into her at *Ringo's*, and she offered to buy me a burger. I had to apologize for losing her the other night at the fair, you know. We did kind of leave her hanging."

"I wasn't about to let her wiggle her way in the middle of any of the rides, and after the drama with David and Paul, everyone kind of scattered, including April." I planted my hands at my waist, still not happy he'd discussed our relationship with my nemesis.

"Simmer down," he said, his voice low and soothing. "She knows where our past relationship stands."

"Which is why she shouldn't insert herself into your life when *our* relationship keeps hitting potholes," I shot back, my voice rising with each word.

Chase's gaze became serious as he replied firmly, "That's exactly why. She's being a friend, just like you are to David, even though you don't have feelings for him anymore."

"Except April still has feelings for you."

"But I don't." His eyes locked with mine, and I struggled to process his words.

"You don't," I repeated, unable to believe it until he confirmed with a slow shake of his head.

"Not the kind she wants from me. April and I are friends, Juli, good friends and nothing more." His words brought an overwhelming sense of relief, but I still couldn't shake off all my doubts.

I stepped back with determination. Simon had seen something important related to David "I have something to tell you."

"Hold on," he interrupted. "I might have told you I understand your reasons, but Julianna, I still don't trust him. If that were me and you, I'd be fighting like hell to get you back."

"But it's not and this isn't about David and me," I reassured him, hoping he could see the sincerity in my words. "This is something Simon told me."

"Simon? What does he have to do with David?" Chase's confusion was evident.

"It's what he saw," I explained, "and I don't know what to do about it because David didn't mention it."

Chase ran a hand through his hair, clearly troubled by this new information. "Spill it, Scarlett."

My heart raced as I revealed the truth. "Simon saw David and Rita in the parking lot of *Pepper's Motel* before the murder."

"Holy cow." Chase's hand fell to his side, his face etched with shock. "This changes a lot of theories."

"Like what? Rita chose Paul." I firmly stood up for my friend, crossing my arms defensively.

Chase glanced around to ensure no one was nearby, then leaned in closer. "I'm going to throw this out there, but it stays between you and me, got it?" His eyes locked onto mine, searching for my agreement.

"Because we're partnering on this case, aren't we?" I challenged, raising an eyebrow.

"No." He shook his head, a slight smile tugging at the corners of his lips.

"Consulting, whatever." I waved my hand dismissively, trying to downplay my eagerness.

"Still no." His smile disappeared, replaced by a serious expression.

"Don't make me regret telling you," I warned, pointing a finger.

"Don't make me lock you up for obstruction of justice." He held up a set of keys, jangling them slightly. "You remember what that was like, right?" His eyes narrowed, testing me.

"You wouldn't." I squared my shoulders, daring him. "Those aren't even the right set of keys," I pointed out, a smirk playing on my lips.

"Don't test me," he replied, his voice stern, but I caught a flicker of amusement in his eyes.

"Spill it, Lawman," I urged, leaning in closer, my curiosity piqued.

"I'm thinking Rita may have chosen Paul as her coverup because she and David are in on this together."

"What? Like they're having an affair? Do you think she secretly wants to be with David? That's not the impression I got when I talked to her."

"What about when you talked with him?"

"That's just it, I believe he really does care about her. Rita told me he said he should never have let her go, which fits with how he acted when he spoke with me."

"Yet you said Rita told him she chose Paul. I don't get it."

"I didn't at first either, but David is respectful. He wouldn't force her to be with him, and he wouldn't hurt her by killing someone she truly loves."

"My theory makes sense from a criminal perspective."

"That's not my David."

"*Your* David?" Chase's brow arched, and I forced out a frustrated breath.

"I mean the David I've known." I snapped my fingers in front of his nose. "Stay focused."

"Let's talk to David and Rita and straighten this out. Something doesn't add up." Chase must have seen the flash of recognition in my eyes because he swiftly corrected, "And by *we*, I mean me and Gary."

"Don't be surprised when David doesn't talk to you. Admit it, you need me."

"I know how to work an investigation. You, Scarlett, are to stay out of this like you were previously ordered to do." Chase leaned forward as if he were about to hug me but pulled back before he got too close. "Dinner at my place? I attempted a southwest veggie burger and sweet potato fries."

"How can I refuse." I smiled, realizing he wasn't over the whole David thing yet, and I couldn't blame him because apparently, I still had April issues.

"It will be early because Gary and I are covering the fair together tonight."

"Sounds good, I'll be there."

After Chase left, I whipped up more baskets to drop off at the fair, I couldn't help but wonder who was watching me and why? I honestly didn't believe Chase thought there was any truth to his theory of David and Rita conspiring to murder. I suppose he needed to rule out even the obvious ideas.

So far, I was the only one who knew they'd met up the morning of the murder. And I still had the pretty young thing angle to work through with David, if he could remember what she looked like.

There was no way I was staying out of this case.

―――――

"How's everything going at the fair?" Chase asked as he plated our burgers and fries. I was impressed by his culinary skills and the fact he was actually going to eat a veggie burger with me.

"Great so far. Andie and Scott keep me updated all day on what the crowd is saying and the items they are short on. This way, I can focus on the kitchen. Would you believe I'm still getting emails and calls from the grand opening?

"I'm really proud of you. I wish you continued success." He clinked his glass of water against my wine glass.

"Thanks. It feels good to be home." I paused a beat before I lost my nerve. "And here with you."

Chase's eyes softened slightly as he heard my words. He paused, a fry halfway to his mouth, and then set it down. He gave a small, thoughtful nod, acknowledging the significance of what I'd said. A flicker of something unspoken passed between us. "Yeah, it's good to have you back," he said, his voice steady, though his eyes hinted at the deeper feelings beneath the surface. Major sat next to me and plopped his fluffy head in my lap. "Major thinks so, too."

"And I've missed him!" I ruffled his mop of fur, and he groaned in contentment. "Did you have a chance to talk to David?"

"I see what you're doing," Chase said with a mouthful of burger, then washed it down before continuing. "You were right. He's not talking, at least to me anyway. I'll have Gary try tomorrow."

"Told you so."

"Well, I did pay a visit to Rita, and she flat out told me she's never been to *Pepper's Motel*. I went to the motel, hoping to look at security camera footage, but they had some glitches in their system so nothing from the last two weeks had recorded. The manager has a call into the company and couldn't give me any more time due to a family of raccoons wreaking havoc on the premises." Chase released an exasperated sigh. "Until I can talk to Simon and get more details, I'm going to believe he was mistaken."

I bit my lower lip in thought, wondering if I should offer up the information about the pretty young woman. "We could have a new person of interest."

"I'm still not ruling out von Hoffster. How do we know he's not trying to pin this on some innocent fairgoer?"

"I—" I began to protest, but then I remembered how effortlessly I could have been set up in the illegal mess Eddie had roped David into back in Boston. I could have easily been the patsy, and my gut told me under Eddie's influence, David would have let it happen.

"What?" Chase asked when I didn't complete my thought.

"Nothing. I'm going to get him to tell me about *Pepper's*. If he wasn't with Rita, or some visiting fairgoer, then who is the mystery woman?"

"Also," Chase continued, "I spoke to Sam about running forensics on this investigation."

"Really? He can do that?"

"Yes. He'll work under the supervision of Rip, as long as he gets approval from his fellowship and can meet the licensing requirements in Connecticut."

"That will be a huge help."

"Speaking of help, I need to meet Gary. You don't mind letting Major out for me, do you?"

"Of course not." I followed him to the door and watched him jog down the front steps. "See you tomorrow, Lawman."

"Good night, Scarlett."

I closed the door and happily cleaned up our dinner dishes. After letting the world's neediest sheepdog out for his evening potty, I locked up and returned to my peaceful house. I made sure to lock up my own doors, and pulled my curtains in case whoever was watching me really was watching. *Why did I even go there?* I'd no sooner flopped onto my couch than my cell phone rang, and I startled, recovering just as quickly as I grinned like crazy at my caller ID.

"Hey, Jules, it's Oliver."

"I know who this is! Your picture comes up on my phone, remember?" We both laughed. "What's going on? You never call me." I sat up straight over my own statement, which was true. I wondered if something was wrong back in Boston.

"I know. I heard about another murder in New Hope, and I wanted to see if you were okay. We all wanted to make sure you weren't involved like the last time."

"Very funny. I was innocently framed." I had been accidentally framed for Pete Seaver's murder. Then later cleared when the real killer showed up. "And, well … I'm kind of involved again."

"Jules, no! What happened? Why didn't you call?"

"Things have been moving fast. Are you sitting down?" I could picture the worry on his face. Ollie was a good egg.

"You're scaring me."

"David is here in New Hope. And he's the lead suspect in this murder." I winced, bracing myself for his reaction.

"Get out! Do you think he did it?"

"No. I'm trying to clear his name so he can get the heck out of my town. And before you throw a thousand questions at me, I've got an odd one for you."

"Go on."

"Have you seen Eddie around the city or hanging around the gallery?"

"Jules, the gallery has been temporarily closed since after you left. I catered for a couple of businesses along the street, and they said about one week after the big event, everything seemed to shut down. No workers, no lights, no art even in the windows."

"Really?" My mind whirled. "I did report him for tax fraud, remember?" I pinched my bottom lip between my teeth.

"I told you not to." Oliver's tone reminded me of Chase, so I shook my head to keep him out of the conversation.

"I couldn't help it; I was so angry over everything." My palm slapped the nearest pillow, then I set it on my lap.

"You had a right to be. We all did. But we should have cooled down and handled things differently."

"I disagree. David needed to be taught a lesson and apparently it worked."

"What do you mean?" Oliver said, while crunching some kind of food in my ear.

"He came to New Hope to find me and try to convince me to return to Boston. What are you eating?"

"He's got some nerve." Oliver laughed. "You seriously didn't think I'd call you to get small-town-murder-tea, without making popcorn, did you?"

"How could I forget your obsession." I giggled. "But there's more."

"I'm all ears."

Oliver and I spoke for over an hour as I caught him up on all of the David drama with Rita, the fight at the fair and incriminating evidence found at the crime scene which led to his arrest, and in turn my current relationship woes.

"You and this Chase guy are finally together, huh?"

"We're working on it." I groaned and flipped over on my back to hug the pillow. "It's such a roller coaster. Right now, he's still upset over me being engaged to David and not telling him."

"Have you told him anything about David? If he cares about you, he kind of has a right to know at least some of the details."

"Every time I try, we always get interrupted. The engagement came as a huge surprise, I get that, and even though he says he understands why I'm defending David; I'm not believing it. I'm sure he's trying to cover the hurt."

"Sure. Knowing you had strong enough feelings for someone to say yes, kind of makes it hard to be all in, right?" Oliver crunched some more, and I suddenly wished I was there with him, sorting out all my issues.

"I guess. But it wasn't like I married the guy."

"Even we guys have to protect our hearts from time to time.

He could be setting himself up for hurt if you choose to go the other way and return to Boston."

"But I'm not." I sat up straight on the couch, suddenly afraid that's how Chase felt. "My business is here. My new life is here. That's why David needs to NOT be here."

"Easy there, Jules, you don't have to convince me."

"I have to convince him." I sighed. "Which is very hard to do when I need to spend so much time working with David to remember any detail that might get him off the hook for murder."

"Yeah, he might be a pompous jerk, but I tend to agree with you. The guy isn't a killer."

"Thank you for believing that, too! I just need some evidence to prove us right."

"Listen, I have a gig at *The Garden* in two days. After that, I'm all yours."

"I appreciate that, Ollie, but for now I'd like to keep my ties to Boston on the down-low, if you get where I'm going."

"Sure."

"Don't take it personally. I have told Chase about all of you. I don't want him asking too many questions."

"You know I trust you, Jules. Call if you need me."

"Thanks, Ollie."

I hung up and lay in silence, thinking about what Oliver had said. While I didn't want Chase to hurt over what happened with David, I wasn't ready to divulge so much of my past all at once. There was a lot of ground to cover and for now I had a clue to follow. Not to mention a dear friend who needed to come clean as much as I did.

It was about time we had another chat.

Nine

The next morning, I attempted to snuggle deeper under the covers but felt resistance. I tugged harder and heard a soft groan. Opening my eyes wide, I slowly turned my head to find a shaggy sheepdog hogging my bed. He rolled to his back, turned his head and licked my cheek.

"Major! What are you doing here?" I propped myself up half thinking I'd see Chase grinning from the doorway. It was just me and Major Floof. "Obviously someone is still on duty." I rolled out of bed, taking a quick peek outside my window in case Scallywag was perched outside. "Whew," I sighed. "Looks like it's you and me. Want a treat?" I walked past the bed as Major bounded past me heading toward the kitchen.

There on the counter was a thermos of coffee and a note from Chase:

Had to leave early. Situation at Rita's salon. Enjoy the coffee and the company. I'll keep you posted on what's happening.
~ C

"Keep me posted?" I smiled when Major's head kinked to the

side. "I swear the man doesn't know me at all. Here, buddy, try one of my peanut butter banana bones, and I'll be right back. You and I are taking a nice w-a-l-k." I grabbed the thermos and headed back upstairs to change.

Moments later, me and my doggie bestie made our way across town to *Nailed It!* salon. I waved at Gary, who seemed to be checking out the perimeter of the building. Once inside the shop, I spotted Chase consoling a very upset Rita from the other side of her nail table.

"What happened?" I looked around but didn't see anything broken or out of place. "Are you okay?" I asked Rita as I took a seat at the glass-top nail station next to hers.

"It's in the back." She sniffed and Major placed a paw of support in her lap. "Thanks, Maj."

"What's in the back?" I glanced at Chase.

"The evidence." Chase said. I'd started to rise when he barked out, "I don't want you going back there. The CSI team is working the zone."

"Then what evidence is back there? Oh my gosh, is there another murder?" I clapped my hand over my mouth at the thought. "Is that it?"

"Juli," Chase warned.

"There's a voodoo doll hanging in the doorway to my studio. I think it's supposed to be me!" She cried and placed her face into her hands.

"A what?" I plopped back into the chair. I must have heard wrong.

"A doll. The same kind of doll you found in your shop." He reached to take my hand. "There was a note."

"Oh, no." I gulped as fear invaded every part of my body. "What did it say?"

"I know what you're doing!" Rita's eyes connected with mine as her uncontrolled tears trailed down her cheeks. "What am I doing? I don't know. Who would even care what I do?"

"I'm wondering the same thing." I glanced between Chase and Rita. "Why the two of us?"

"You're friends." Chase pointed at each of us. "Easy to pit one of you against the other or use one of you as leverage to get what they want from the other person."

"Get what they want?" Rita wiped her tears. "What could we possibly have?"

"You both share one common bond."

"David." Our voices were whispers we both heard, as recognition dawned. "What?"

"You were married to him, still are as a matter of fact," I addressed Rita. "I was only briefly engaged."

"We haven't had any contact until he came here to find you." She pointed toward me, then focused on Chase. "As I've said before, I was in love with Paul. I was marrying Paul."

"Then what could be connecting you two if it isn't David?" Chase's voice was sharp as he pulled out his trusty notebook, his brow furrowing with concern.

"Maybe it's Juli's painting?" Rita alleged her tone dripping with an accusation which made my stomach churn.

"My—" I stammered, feeling a wave of unease.

"Painting?" Chase turned his full attention to me, his eyes piercing through my hesitation.

"What about yours?" I shot back, pointed a finger at Rita, my heart pounding in my chest.

"I'm assuming he gave you that Oscar as an engagement gift?" Rita's eyes widened with realization.

"Great, an engagement gift." Chase grumbled, his voice laced with frustration. His jaw tightened as he glanced between us.

"Now I know he gave you *your* Oscar, too," My voice trembling with a mix of anger and betrayal.

"Who or what is this Oscar? One of you better start explaining," Chase demanded, his patience wearing thin. His gaze a daunting blend of confusion and determination.

"Oscar Royce is an artist," I said, my voice soft and informative. The name hung in the air, heavy with unspoken history and tangled emotions.

"David is very fond of his work," Rita added. "He gave me a painting on our wedding night, and it's remained one of my favorites. I have it hanging in my home."

"And what about yours?" Chase rested his forearms on the nail table as he questioned me. "I don't think I've seen anything new hanging on the walls of your house or your shop."

"Because I have it," Rita admitted and for that I was thankful. "Juli commissioned me to use it to make a stained glass copy so she could display it."

"Why not hang it in the house like Rita?" His question was innocent enough.

Oh boy, this was not the way I wanted to discuss this. Chase once again waited patiently for me to answer and this time I had the privilege of having Rita's eyes on me as well. I couldn't tell them the truth. Yes, technically I stole it from the gallery, but I'd earned it. Neither of them would understand.

"The memory is still too painful for me." I glanced away from their curious eyes, praying my lawman would buy in. "I'd met the artist personally and thought the stained glass would bring new life to the piece and start to hold new memories." There, that seemed to come off well. Or so I thought.

"I'm not buying it." Chase sat back in the chair, locking eyes with me.

My eyes pleaded with his to just let this go. Of course, he was in prime Sheriff-Goody mode. Just my luck.

"I think there's more to this painting and to your time in Boston that you continue to keep from me."

"Chase, I promise I will tell you everything you want to know. Now is not the time."

"You're right, Julianna, it's not the time. Only it shouldn't have gotten to this point." Again, he was right. Sometimes I wish he wasn't so good at what he did. "I need to finish up here with Gary. Why don't you take Major to your shop for a while. We'll talk later."

"I'd like to stay." I still had questions for Rita.

"And I asked you to go." Again, with the formal tone. "Oh, but before you do … if I find out you're holding back information detrimental to this case, I *will* arrest you."

I opened my mouth to protest and quickly clamped it shut. I knew better than to argue. I would choose my battles. There was also a delivery to be made to the fairgrounds and a chance to find the pretty young woman myself.

———

ONCE I GOT TO THE FAIRGROUNDS, I DROPPED OFF FRESH samples and more packages of goods to my tent. With all the visitors being trapped in town, business was booming, and I'd enlisted Betty and Mrs. B to help fulfill orders and pre-package samples. Scott and Andie were off on the midway rides, so Betty and Tammy had taken over for a while. They were the perfect substitutes. Both women were very chatty and could sell snow to an Eskimo.

"So glad to see you, darlin'," Betty stood from the lawn chair and gave me a big hug. "We're just about out of the BisScotties and those sweet little cinnamon twists."

"Not to mention the Kitty Krackers," Tammy added. "Juli, your shop is becoming the talk of the county!"

"Thanks so much, ladies. I really appreciate you helping relieve the kids."

"It's no trouble at all. I like watching Andie with a nice boy like Scott. I'm sure you know my niece has been a handful for a while now."

"I heard. It was obvious Max Perez had been taking advantage of her. And if you ask me, Scott is falling fast."

"I'd have to agree. I've seen great changes in our girl as their relationship has developed." Tammy all but glowed.

"They work so well together at the café. I'm glad they're not too bored here."

"Thank you for giving her a chance."

"You're welcome, Tammy. I'm hoping they can keep some of their hours once school starts. I'd hate to lose them completely."

"And those two kids are not bored at all." Betty talked louder than Tammy. "Why, they've been selling to their friends and have no problems striking conversation with anyone who walks up."

"That's fantastic. Obviously, Andie has been a great influence on Scott. He always seemed so shy." I straightened up some displays and glanced over at Rita's tent. Everything had been packed up. I felt bad that she didn't stay. Then again, I had no idea what she was really going through. I still wanted to talk to her.

"So sad about Paul and Rita," Tammy said as if reading my thoughts.

"Such a nice young man and they were so happy," Betty added.

"I know. My heart hurts so much for her."

"Does the sheriff have any leads? What about that David fella? Rumor has it you know him."

"I do, from back in Boston." I swallowed the lump in my throat. I hoped they hadn't heard everything. I just didn't want to discuss it with the two busiest busy bodies in New Hope. "I worked for him at an art gallery."

"He didn't take advantage of you did he, sweet pea?"

"No." I gave Betty a wistful smile. "When I found out Mom had died, I knew I had to come home. It was time to leave."

"Bless your heart, sugar. Your mama would be so proud of you and everything you've done since coming home."

"This town sure did miss you, Juli," Tammy added while Betty nodded in agreement.

"Thanks, ladies, again for everything. I have a couple other people I need to see so I'm going to scoot." I waved and continued my journey toward the *Fit-Fanatics* tent.

The tent was situated at the very end of the row with a view of what is known as the Grand Stage, where they hold talent competitions, local musicians play, and of course, where they were going to hold the body building competition. Sandy must have charged them a pretty penny for their spot. I couldn't even imagine how much money they must have paid for everything they had hauled into the tent and the signage in front of it.

I had to admit, I was impressed. They had thought of everything. Sign-up sheets for their newsletter, gym membership registrations, competition sign ups, and even personal consultations on nutrition and training. All I had thought to do for my business was samples and sellable products. Although something told me the genius behind a lot of this was Rita.

As I stepped into the tent, I couldn't help but overhear a conversation Ivan was having with an extremely good-looking and very fit couple. Both were tall and lean. They didn't strike me as body builders. They wore black fitness apparel, baring a large, lime green "T". The couple didn't look very happy, and Ivan seemed a little annoyed. I casually browsed some literature and signed up for their newsletter, hoping to gather some information.

"Listen, Ivan," the woman said, her rich golden ponytail falling over her shoulder as she leaned forward on his table, "we had a deal, and your partner reneged on it."

"I'm sorry but given the circumstances of his death, I am unable to continue with our sponsorship."

"You agreed to represent our supplement line. We made a deal." The man stepped forward and I thought for sure he was going to strike Ivan, except for the bandage on his left hand.

"We did. That deal, may I remind you, was contingent on my partner also being in agreement. He was not, and I didn't have enough time before he was murdered to try to convince him."

Or did Ivan kill him because Paul wouldn't agree with what Ivan wanted? My mind spun with possibilities.

"Erik tried to convince him, and he wouldn't budge." The woman moved next to the man. "He said he had already been contacted by a competitor and was getting better commission margins with them. He never even knew what we were offering." The woman's voice became loud and shrill.

"Which means you never spoke with him." The man leaned in close to Ivan's round face.

The plot thickened. I strained to hear more.

"Erik, Sheila, the timing is not right. I need time to settle the gym and this awful idea of expansion. When I'm back at our gym, I'll reach out to you again and we'll re-negotiate. My hands are tied right now. I have a lot to do to dissolve Paul's side of the business. I don't know how long that will take. I've already contacted my lawyer."

"Good, because an agreement is an agreement. We are well known in the industry, Ivan. We can ruin your reputation in a heartbeat. I tried to explain that to Paul the other night, but he was not as understanding as you." Erik raised his bandaged hand. "I told him it would be his own demise if he didn't honor what you started with us."

I sucked in a sharp breath and pressed my lips together, pretending to look around. Could they have killed him for saying no?

"Don't worry, Sheila." Erik put her arm around her. "Ivan knows our reputation. He will be partnering with the right company." Erik extended his hand, and Ivan shook it without question.

"We'll be in touch." Sheila turned and bumped into me. "Here," she reached into her bag and pulled out a coupon. "Take this, it's better than any deal they have here right now. Best supplement for good health you will ever need."

I looked into her captivating golden eyes that eerily matched her golden hair. What if she was the one? The mysterious woman David saw. I had to act fast.

"Oh my gosh, you're the Tullersons!" I'd read their names on the coupon and for once didn't blow an opportunity. "Could I please get a picture? I've seen you both on social media. You're amazing, and I've always wanted to try your products."

"Of course. Erik get in the photo," Sheila ordered. They stood behind me, and I quickly snapped the selfie. Chase would be proud of me for this one.

"Thank you so much," I called to them as they exited the tent. "Wow, they are intense," I said to Ivan as I neared his table.

"You can say that again. What brings you by?" He eyed me curiously as I'm sure he could tell I'd never worked out or taken any kind of supplement in my life.

"Sorry, I couldn't help but overhearing. Is everything okay with the gym? I know Paul was really excited about the expansion."

"No, it's not all right. I told him this was a stupid idea to begin with. We always wanted to remain a boutique facility with a more personalized experience. I knew if I agreed to this then he'd want to expand further. That wasn't our vision."

"Visions can change." Boy, didn't I know it. "It's okay to try new things."

"It is for some people, but not me. I'm sorry Paul is dead, but now I can keep the business running the way I want it to be run. Forget this expansion nonsense."

"Was Sheila Tullerson the one you had hired as the manager for the new gym?"

Ivan narrowed his eyes and studied me. "Let me guess, Rita's running her mouth again? I told Paul not to tell her about our business decisions. She sticks her nose where it doesn't belong and influences him far too much. He was better off before he met her."

"She loved him very much."

"Of course she did. To answer your question, no. Sheila

Tullerson is a media giant and someone we should be partnering with. The manager we were having problems with is Fawn Wilson."

"Then you're not having problems with her? Must be Paul straightened everything out?"

"No, he didn't. I had to jump into that arena too. Looks like he failed to tell Rita about his prior relationship with Fawn."

"I guess he never got the chance." I refused to believe Paul had kept secrets from Rita. Then again, I was in no position to think about other people's secrets.

"Oh, he's had more than enough chances. And this time Fawn was calling the shots."

"What do you mean?" My worry meter spiked, and I suddenly wished Chase was with me. I felt like I was on to something or getting close, and Ivan seemed pretty angry about the whole thing.

"Paul trained her and got her into the circuit. She's built perfectly for it. Then, she disappeared. I think they were involved somehow. He took her leaving him pretty hard. In time, he got over her and met Rita. Right when he's getting out of his slump, Fawn magically appears, wanting to get back into the game and back into his life."

"I guarantee Rita didn't know that." Could Fawn be a suspect as well? She couldn't have been happy when Paul turned her down.

"And that's all I'm saying. She demanded he give her a job and train her again. Paul was ready to give in until I stepped in and fired her before she could take the job. We don't need this kind of drama. I told him it was bad business."

"Of course." I slowly stepped backward toward the exit. Ivan had some issues with Paul, and I began to wonder if he was angry enough with him to kill him. "Oops! Look at that, I have an appointment. Nice talking to you Ivan." I waved and walked out as fast as I could.

In one quick meeting I had more suspects than I'd intended

and a selfie with a person of interest. Everyone had a fight with Paul, and in my mind, a motive for murder.

Ten

The next morning it was my turn to knock on Chase's door. When he answered, I presented him with a basket of breakfast items. I could smell the fresh brewed coffee as I walked through the house and smiled. My lawman was so predictable. And so sexy in a pair of faded blue jeans and classic white t-shirt, padding barefoot across the hardwood floor.

"I'm glad you came over, and not just for the food."

"Believe it or not, I miss this big lug." I set the basket on the table and reached into the oversized pocket of my teal sundress, sprinkled with dainty white flowers, and pulled out a small baggie of bone shaped cookies for Major. As he gently took a biscuit from my hand, I glanced at Chase.

He poured two large mugs of coffee, and I watched him add cream to mine. "You know you're spoiling him." Chase nodded toward the baggie as I set it on the counter. "I can tell he misses you, too."

"I have to tell you what I found out." I began unpacking items from my basket while Chase set the table.

Chase stopped short, as if just then hearing what I said. "Wait, found out? Found out what? Were you investigating this case? Julianna, you need to stay out of it."

"I know, but I was at the fairgrounds, and I ran into Ivan. Only he wasn't alone, and I overheard a conversation with the Tullersons."

"And they are ..."

"Some fitness people who have a supplement line. From what I gathered they had approached Ivan, who was all for it, but then Paul didn't want to go in with them. I guess they got into a fight with Paul, telling him he would regret it, and are now going back to Ivan to make good with the deal."

"That's a lot of overhearing."

"Oh wait, there's more."

"Did you question the entire town in one afternoon? Tell me you didn't do anything illegal."

"No. I merely took good mental notes, and I had a conversation with Ivan after they left. Come to find out, the manager they were having a problem with used to be in a relationship with Paul."

"And the plot thickens." Chase set a warm banana nut muffin on his plate and a blueberry one on mine.

"It sure does. Ivan became really agitated over the whole thing, too. I guess Paul trained some woman named Fawn, and she did great on the bodybuilding circuit. He said he was pretty sure they were involved outside of training. Then she suddenly disappeared with no contact. Paul was devastated, and then he met Rita."

"This woman Fawn, she was the manager?"

"Yes. She recently returned and began making all sorts of demands on Paul. She was forcing him to give her the manager job at the new gym and also that he start training her again."

"And you think the supplement people and the ex-lover are suspects."

"Yes. The Tullersons, Fawn and Ivan. Chase, you didn't see how angry and loud Ivan became while talking about all the drama with Paul. He never wanted to expand the gym. He even said that he's sorry Paul is dead, but now he can renegotiate and run the gym the way he wants to. He said Paul lost sight of their vision and blames Rita."

"Rita isn't blaming anyone, but I do think she's protecting someone. She was very evasive when I probed her more about the doll and, of course, her relationship with David."

"Yeah, I was getting the same feeling. I actually wanted to talk to her yesterday about the doll, but you were there."

"Let's discuss the doll, shall we?"

"You think they are connected?"

"Maybe. I'm confident the contributing factor is von Hoffster. My burning question is why, and I think dear Scarlett, you know the answer to that."

Here it was, my do or die moment. I'd just handed him four plausible suspects, surely, he wouldn't be too upset with me for taking what was owed to me. Then again, how patient could he be?

"Juli, if we're ever going to move forward, we need to put the past behind us. I'm trying to get there, but there are things I need to know."

"Then take off your sheriff hat because I won't have you judging me. You don't know what I went through."

"Tell me." His eyes clouded with determination. "Then if I have to, I will put that man away for more than tax fraud."

"No!"

"No?" Pure confusion covered his face.

"I reported him for tax fraud out of spite. He doesn't deserve to go to jail, especially for murder. He didn't kill Paul, and this stupid doll thing has got me stumped. It's not like him. David doesn't use scare tactics. He has—"

"He has what?"

"People to do it for him."

"People like who?" Chase slid his muffin to the side.

"Eddie, this guy who worked at the gallery. He was so shady all the time. I tried to tell David, but he didn't believe me, he said I was overreacting. He kept him on and started giving him responsibilities that were mine. I didn't trust him, so I spied on him in the warehouse. That's when I saw him taking the backing off the paintings, putting in blocks of drugs and then replacing the backing. After that, I knew I needed to get out."

"Wait, drugs? Julianna, what kind of trouble did you get into? Who are these art people friends you have? You never should have gone away."

"I needed to go away, and you know it. I couldn't have stayed here."

"Yes, you could." We sat in silence for a moment before he said, "What do these drug people want from you? Don't tell me you have their drugs."

"No. I took a painting. *Lost Horizon*, by Oscar. Everything I said at Rita's was true. I met the artist, and I love his work. Except David didn't give it to me. I stole it before they could use it to smuggle drugs in the back of the frame. My relationship with David was over. He owed me so much money, I had to ensure that I'd get it, and the painting was the only way."

"Does David know you have the painting?"

"Yes. I believe that's why he came to New Hope. Only he didn't plan on finding Rita here, too. She's become his distraction, at least for now."

"If he presses charges, you do realize I'd have to arrest you."

"Are you serious? Chase, after all I've done to help him, he'd be foolish to press charges. Right?"

"I'm just putting it out there. Where is the painting now?"

"It's in Rita's safe while she works on the stained glass version. Do you think that's why she got a doll, too?"

"It seems to make sense. But who knew you had the painting other than you and David?"

"My friends back in Boston, no one here. Rita didn't know

until I showed up with it." I paused then snapped my fingers. "Simon Banks! I accidentally bumped into him while walking down the sidewalk on my way to see Rita. I had the painting in a tube. The cap fell off when we collided and he replaced it."

"Did he see the painting?"

"No, only I did tell him it was a painting. He'd have no way to know exactly which one it was."

"Interesting how he came to town shortly before you did. Do you recognize him at all?"

"I hadn't thought of that. And no, I don't recognize him. I've never seen his eyes, but just off of appearance and build, he doesn't ring a bell. I briefly met Simon Percy when I was with David. We did a lot of work with his family's auction house, but he didn't look at all like Simon Banks."

"Unfortunately, I think we're back to square one with the dolls until we can figure out who wants your painting, other than David."

"There must be something Rita has as well, right? Why scare her with a doll, unless they want her painting too?"

"They could, if they found out she has one."

"Looks like you have two different cases going on." I blew across my coffee mug and took a sip.

"We're going to need to evaluate all these suspects."

"Of course, where are we going to start? I say we hit the gym."

"You don't work out. Remember you ended up in the hospital from jogging."

"I was attacked, and I've gotten better. I want to help."

"I think it's best you let me and Gary handle things going forward. You're too involved with David, and now there's the whole painting angle to worry about."

"You know I'm not going to listen."

"I can only hope."

"Chase!" Gary appeared in the kitchen. "Oh, hey, Juli. Did you bring muffins?" He proceeded to pour a cup of coffee, grabbed a muffin, and sat down at the table.

"Do you ever knock?" Chase grumbled.

"I did and even rang the bell. Sorry, Boss, but it couldn't wait."

"Go on."

"First, these blueberry muffins are amazing, Juli. Seriously, Boss, if you don't do something soon, I will. You can't let her go."

"Watch yourself, Deputy, or I'll ship you back to Detroit."

"Sorry, Chase but Juli is—"

"Yes, I know, she's amazing." He glanced my way and winked. My heart did its usual rapid flutter, and I winked back. He'd surprisingly handled the whole painting thing better than I thought. Which led me to believe he wasn't handling it at all. "Get to the point, Gary."

"I spoke to Simon, and he pegged both David and Rita from some photos I showed him."

"Which means they're both lying." Chase ground out.

"Or trying to protect each other." Gary said between a mouthful of an orange cranberry muffin. "Mmm-amazing."

"You can't think one of them actually killed Paul!" I jumped to my feet. "Rita and Paul were in love and planning a future. David is ... well, he's just David and even if he really does love Rita, you don't come to town and plan a murder."

"Some people do, Juli," Gary said, and I wanted to smack him.

"Not helping, Gary."

"Maybe they didn't intend to, but you have to admit they are the most likely suspects right now," Chase stated. "Which means we need to bring Rita in for questioning."

I plopped back into the chair, not wanting to believe either of them capable of murder, yet wondering if they'd gotten into something over their heads and murder was the only way out.

———

I paced anxiously in Chase's living room, waiting for news about Rita's questioning. Despite my protests, Chase had insisted on bringing her in for a formal interview at the station. I hated the thought of my friend being treated like a suspect. After what felt like hours, I heard the front door open. Chase walked in, looking tired.

"Well?" I asked immediately. "How did it go?"

Chase sighed and ran a hand through his hair. "She's sticking to her story. Says she never met David at *Pepper's Motel*."

"Do you believe her?"

"I don't know what to believe at this point," Chase admitted. "Her alibi for the night of Paul's murder checks out—she was home alone, but neighbors confirm seeing her lights on late into the night. And she seems genuinely devastated about Paul."

I nodded, relieved Rita hadn't been arrested. "So, what now?"

Chase sat down heavily on the couch. "We keep digging. There are still a lot of unanswered questions. We're still looking into Erik and Sheila Tullerson, and Gary is trying to track down Fawn Wilson for questioning.

"And David?" I asked hesitantly as I sat next to Chase.

"He's still our prime suspect. His alibi is shaky and there's no witness to confirm. We're still waiting on forensics."

"The Tullersons are tops on my list. They certainly had motive if Paul was backing out of their deal."

"Hold up. *Your* list?" Chase's brow arched high.

"*Our* list?" I squeaked. "Partner?"

"No." He rose from the couch.

"Consultant," I firmly corrected, tucking my thick waves behind my ear.

"Still no."

"Why not?" I stood directly behind him. Now was not the time for him to be unreasonable. "Between the three of us we can cover a lot of ground and get to the bottom of things sooner."

"Three of us." He turned to face me, massaging the scruff of hair along his chin.

"I'm adding Gary to our dynamic duo. C'mon, Chase. You've got Liam to mind the station which frees Gary to help us solve this case. More eyes open and feet on the ground. Seems solid to me."

"Juli, I need you to promise me something."

I tensed, knowing what was coming but opted to play dumb. "What?"

"I need you to step back from this investigation. I'm still not comfortable with the threats against you and Rita, and I somehow think they are connected to what happened to Paul. It's too coincidental. Let me and my team handle this."

I opened my mouth to protest, but Chase's phone rang. He held up a hand to stop me as he walked into another room to take the call. Of course I followed.

"Gary, what's up?" Chase shook his head in my direction then focused on what Gary was saying. "What? Is he sure? Okay, I'm on my way."

"What's going on?" I trailed behind Chase as he grabbed his hat and keys. Major followed as if on cue, fussing the entire way to the kitchen. I glanced over my shoulder at the giant fluff ball. "What's up with him?"

"Sam is working with Rip on the forensics." Chase reached into the freezer and pulled out what looked to be a large rubber toy. "He wants this." He handed it to the giant baby who happily pranced back into the living room.

"What is that and why haven't you given me this secret for such magic to calm him down and keep him out of my hair?"

"I fill it with a small amount of his kibble and yogurt with peanut butter on both ends. I freeze it and give it to him when I know I won't be back for a while. It's his special treat."

"Noted." I gazed at the contented canine and then back to Chase. "I take it Sam has information?"

"He does." Chase motioned me out the door first so he could lock up.

"Spill it." I jabbed my hands at my waist, taking a stance.

"Don't you have baking to do? Customer orders to fulfill?" He shoved the keys in his pocket.

"A case to solve?" I added, with a playful smile.

"*I* have the case to solve." He pointed at me and said, "Chaos," then pointed to himself, "Justice."

"Unbelievable." I passed him going down the steps. "Why are you wasting time?"

"You two headed to the fair? It's a lovely night," Mrs. Bailey called from her front porch. She and her sister, Wanda, sat with a plate of cookies and pitcher of tea between them, the scent of vanilla and sugar sifting through the air.

"Work," both Chase and I spoke in unison, our synchronized reply making us exchange an amused glance.

"Don't work too hard, now. Make room for some fun." The old woman gave us a wink, her eyes twinkling with mischief, as if I couldn't read between the lines already.

"Always, Mrs. B!" I called back, waving cheerfully.

"Of course, Ida," Chase replied, his voice carrying a hint of nostalgia. He then shot me a knowing look, one that transported me back to simpler times when fun was all that mattered. His expression softened, the corners of his mustache twitching upward in a half-smile, and for a brief moment, the weight of the present seemed to lift.

Only there was no time for fun, not until we solved this case.

oments later we arrived at the station. Sam and Gary were waiting in Chase's office. I closed the door once I was inside, and all three men stared. Chase, most of all, knew I wasn't leaving.

"She's fine, gentlemen." He pointed a finger at me in warning. "What's said in this room, stays in this room, got it?"

I nodded.

"This is no game, Julianna. If you want to clear your boyfriend's name, then there can be no leaks of information."

I winced a little at the *boyfriend* remark. Apparently, he was still angry with me.

"What do we have, Sam?"

"Paul's injuries did not kill him. The bruises from the fight with David were minimal at best. He did sustain new bruising when he fell, but nothing too impactful as to cause his death."

"Then David couldn't have killed him." My words came out on a whisper.

"Don't be so sure," Chase reminded me with a slight growl to his voice. "He's a suspect for a reason."

"What do you think was the cause of death?" Gary calmly asked, and I was thankful for the change of subject.

"Hyperglycemic hyperosmolar nonketotic coma." Sam paused over our confused expressions. "Oh, sorry. Basically, a diabetic coma."

"But he had his insulin. Did he not take it in time?" I questioned, trying to connect the dots that hopefully led away from David.

"Yeah, Sam, the injector pen was next to him. From what I saw without disturbing anything, it was empty." Gary shoved his hands in his pockets, his brows pinching together in thought.

"There was no insulin in his blood stream. Toxicology did detect trace amounts of steroids."

"You mean, he passed out before he could inject himself?" Chase perched on the corner of his desk. "Did he miss?"

"He injected. There was a small puncture mark on the skin of his abdomen." Sam stood before us like a proud teacher about to explain something we didn't understand. "Sometimes, it can take up to thirty minutes for the effects of the insulin to be felt. If his blood sugar was too high, he shouldn't have been alone. He should have been taken to the hospital."

"Maybe he wasn't alone." Chase's intense green eyes met mine.

"No. David said he paid a visit and left because Paul wanted to fight again."

"Look at the signs, Juli. He could have very well come back. A piece of his shirt was at the crime scene."

"It doesn't matter," Sam interjected. "Paul's pen used replaceable cartridges. Upon further inspection and testing, we found the fluid remnants in the cartridge to be nothing more than simple saline."

"Someone knew what they were doing." Chase furrowed his brows, drumming his fingers on his knee.

"I would tend to agree. The dosage knob had been manipulated to deliver the maximum amount, which in this case was only saline."

"Why go through all that trouble if it was just saline?" I asked. "Maybe they didn't mean to kill him."

"Saline and insulin look like the same, clear liquid," Sam explained. "Paul wouldn't have known anything had been tampered with."

"Paul seemed okay when we first met up. I remember Rita asking him about his insulin, and he said he'd go get it," I mused, trying to remember if anything seemed out of the ordinary.

"But he never had the chance," Chase interjected. "David showed up and all hell broke loose."

"I wish you'd stop pointing the finger at him." I scowled.

"I wish you'd stop defending him," Chase barked back.

"Because I know he's innocent. *You're* just being stubborn." I couldn't keep the exasperation out of my voice. I crossed my arms, my gaze challenging as I declared, "You don't know him like I do."

Chase's green eyes flashed with annoyance. "Nor do I want to. I'm being thorough, Juli. It's my job to consider every possibility."

"And it's my job to stand up and support my friends." I lifted my chin in defiance. "I think you're letting your personal feelings cloud your judgment."

The tension between us crackled in the air, years of history and unresolved feelings adding fuel to a disagreement I began to think we'd never be able to move past. Somewhere in the distance I heard Gary clear his throat and Sam scuff a sneaker across the laminate floor.

Chase ran a hand through his hair, his expression a mix of concern and irritation. "You must admit his timing is suspicious. He shows up out of nowhere right when Paul ..." Chase trailed off when his office door drifted open. All our eyes darted to Rita, who stood in the doorway, her face a mask of grief and determination.

"Why are you all in here?"

"Rita." Chase hopped off the edge of his desk and approached, but she backed out of the door.

"You, you should be out there!" She pointed toward the door to the station. "Out there trying to find the killer. Paul is dead and all you can do is bicker amongst each other. What kind of sheriff are you?"

"We're working on it, Ms. Davis." Gary stepped forward.

"Are you?" Her dark brown eyes bore into each of us with a fierce intensity, each glance laced with palpable anger and accusation. "An innocent man is behind bars, and you're doing nothing."

"You and Juli seem to know more about our guest than I do. Please understand, we have too many unanswered questions." Chase kept his voice calm even though Rita's appearance added another layer to his frustration. "My instincts tell me there's more to that man than meets the eye. I don't think either of you know what he's fully capable of."

"Then enlighten me, Sheriff," David's smooth voice filtered into Chase's office. "What exactly am I capable of?"

Rita marched toward the jail cell, and we all followed. My worry meter clicked on. Rita appeared more than scattered. Something bad was about to happen. Thank goodness she wore leggings and a T-shirt. There was nowhere she could hide a weapon.

"This man did not kill Paul Rivera!" she declared, stepping up to the bars of the cell.

"Shh ... Rita, it's going to be okay."

"No, David, I can't do this anymore." Rita began to cry, sinking to the floor with her hands covering her face. "I've tried to forget, but I can't."

"Shhh ..." David cooed, trying to console her. My stomach twisted as a strange thought entered my mind.

"I know what we talked about," Rita began between sobs, "but I can't keep the secret. I can't lie. Please, I can't do it any longer."

"Rita, what are you saying?" I crouched in front of her with my hand on her knees. I looked up at David's concerned face, then over at Gary and Chase who seemed confused, until Chase picked up on my thoughts and thankfully voiced them because I couldn't.

"Rita, did you kill Paul?"

"What?" David yelled and jumped to his feet.

"No!" Rita wiped her face and glanced at David as if for direction. I felt the vibration of the room switch to something darker, heavier. The air seemed to thicken with secrets as everyone waited for her next words. "David is innocent and I'm going to tell you why."

"Rita, darling, don't."

"Shh! David!" My brisk command broke their tender moment.

Chase shot me a sharp, questioning glare, his eyes narrowing in suspicion and curiosity. The tension in his face was evident, as though trying to read between the lines of my outburst, searching for hidden truths.

"Rita, please, continue." Chase focused on her, for which I was grateful. A sudden wave of disorientation hit me as I realized just how much was left unsaid between Chase and me.

"David didn't kill Paul." Rita paused and looked at me. "I'm so sorry, Juli. I wasn't truthful with you. I didn't tell you everything, and you were being so honest with me."

David's voice held a soft warning tone. "Rita ..."

"No, David, it's okay. This needs to be said. I'm tired of keeping to myself and staying quiet. I had the chance to stop this sooner when Juli and I were talking."

"And when was this?" Sherrif nosey britches chimed in, and I snapped my head in his direction. He held my stare until Rita started talking.

"The day I saw you all at *Ringo's*. I came to pick up a breakfast order."

"The day Paul was found at the fairgrounds."

"Yes." She nodded and touched fingers with David through the steel bars of his cell. "As I told Juli, the breakfast was for David and me. While I'd explained we had been talking most of the night, what I didn't tell her was that David stayed with me that night. We woke up together, and I offered to go grab breakfast so we could continue our conversations."

"Let me get this straight," Chase said, pointing toward the cell, "David was with you all night?"

"Yes."

"What about Paul?"

"He was still very angry with me for keeping my past with David a secret. He planned on staying at Ivan's hotel because they were still working on a problem with one of their managers. He told me he needed time to cool off."

"You told me both of you ended by saying you loved each other," I reminded her.

"We did. You can think what you want, but that didn't stop me from talking to David."

"Or asking me to stay," David said and blew her a kiss.

I waved my arms in a halting gesture. "Wait just a minute. When did you get to Rita's?" I asked David, who stood grinning like a Cheshire cat.

"Jealous, darling?"

"David!" Rita admonished.

"No!" I shook my head, still trying to process everything. "I'm only trying to figure out your timeline."

"Same here," Chase added. "For all we know, von Hoffster, you could have messed with Paul's insulin before he wanted to fight you, then you left to save face and act like the bigger man."

"Except I didn't, sheriff. Maybe you should be searching for the hot blonde muscle chick who entered his tent after me. Juli tried to get more details from me, but I honestly don't recall her features. All I can say is she was fired up about something."

"Not helping, David." I pressed my lips together to keep myself from screaming.

"You knew about this?" The shock registering across Chase's features caused me to catch my breath.

"I was going to tell you."

"Right," Chase ground out, barely making eye contact.

"What are we going to do with him, Boss?" Gary asked.

"Now that Rita has come forward as your alibi, we're letting you go, von Hoffster."

"Oh, thank you, Chase!" Rita jumped forward and gave him a hug. "See, David, I knew we could trust them. There was no reason for you to stay in this cell a moment longer."

"Tell me this, why were you being the fall guy?" Chase stepped forward and unlocked the cell. "Why wouldn't you want Rita to come forward sooner?"

"Because, dear Sheriff, I care about her very much. I knew how implicating it would be for her. She admitted to fighting with Rivera. For all you knew, we could have been in on it together." David shrugged, and Chase grumbled something inaudible.

"This town is still in a lockdown, so don't even attempt to go anywhere," He announced while crossing the room to hang up the keys.

"It's okay, he'll be staying with me," Rita said as she looped her arm through David's, and I couldn't hide the bewilderment from my face, which brought amusement to David's. I tried to be impartial, but it baffled me how Rita's feelings could shift so abruptly from Paul to David.

"I can't wait." David scrubbed a hand across his face and through his sandy brown hair. "These conditions are deplorable. I most definitely need a shower."

Chase stopped them by placing his palm on David's chest. "Keep your nose clean. I still don't trust you, and I'd bet money you're hiding something."

"Sheriff Hargrave, I'm not hiding anything. I suggest you sharpen your skills because everything is right under your nose." David elegantly removed Chase's hand. "Now, if you'll excuse me, I'd like my belongings so I can destress with a nice Chianti."

"Gary, get his things from the locker. Stay out of trouble, von Hoffster."

"Wow, can you believe it?" I closed the station door after Rita and David left. "Rita of all people is David's alibi."

Chase leaned against his desk; his brows furrowed in frustration. He was a steady presence, but today he seemed on edge, like a coiled spring ready to snap. "Why didn't you tell me any of this?" His voice cut through my thoughts, taut and serious. "I am running the investigations, not you."

I pushed myself away from the door, pacing across the worn vinyl flooring. "You know how Rita is. She's—"

"That doesn't matter," he interrupted, exasperation evident in his voice. "I've asked you to stay out of this for your own safety, yet you don't listen." I watched the rise and fall of his chest as he released a sigh. "This isn't just some mystery to solve. It's real lives on the line."

I felt my cheeks flush with heat. "I'm trying to help."

"Help?" he echoed, disbelief etched into his features. "Is keeping secrets helping? Because that's what you seem to be doing."

"Is this going to turn into that whole obstruction of justice thing?" I said, my agitation bubbling over. "Because if it is, you can stop right there."

Chase stood across from me, arms crossed tightly over his chest, jaw muscles clenched. The authority he wore like armor faltered against a tide of doubt and vulnerability. His eyes, usually so clear and decisive, now seemed shaded in turmoil. "You think this is a joke?" his voice wavered, betraying the tension beneath his stern façade.

"No, I'm serious!" My voice rose, and I took a breath to steady myself. "I was waiting to see if I could get more clues on my own. Then I could present them to you, and we could go after them together."

His eyes narrowed, and a flicker of something akin to disappointment passed through them. "A true partner doesn't keep information for themselves," he shot back, his tone clipped but laced with concern.

My heart in my chest, the reality of our situation crashed over me. We weren't just two people working on a case, we were tangled in something deeper, clouded by history and unspoken feelings. The silence stretched between us, heavy with possibilities. Outside the world moved on, the cheerful buzz of townsfolk, visitors enjoying the excitement of the county fair. But here, in this moment, everything felt suspended, balanced on the knife's edge of our confrontation.

"Scarlett," Chase's voice broke into my thoughts. He stepped closer, his expression shifting from irritation to something softer. "I need you to be straight with me." His eyes narrowed slightly, focusing intently on mine. "Is there anything else you know about David that could be relevant? Anything at all about his business dealings or connections that seem shady?"

I chewed my lip, debating how much to reveal. Sure, there were lots of things, but they wouldn't make sense because there had never been a good time to let Chase in. Now wasn't the time, either.

"Julianna ..." His tone softened. "This is about trust."

"No, there's nothing I can think of."

The silence that followed felt suffocating, thickening as I wrestled with my tangled emotions. Trust. That word hung heavy between us. Could I truly share everything? Would he still look at me the same if he peeled back the layers to all my doubts and fears?

"Trust goes both ways," I finally whispered. I wanted to believe we could face anything together, but one thing after another cast shadows over us to the point where we lost track of who we were individually as well as together.

"I can't keep doing this," he continued, his tone dropping to an exasperated sigh. "I'm trying, but you refuse to even meet me halfway."

"That's not fair," I protested. "I have my reasons."

"Reasons? Or excuses?" He took a step back, running a hand through his tousled hair, clearly struggling with himself. "For both our sakes, we need some space, a break."

"A break?" My voice shattered, disbelief and a wave of hurt crashing over me. My heart ached, each beat a painful reminder of what this could mean. "Is that really what you want?" My eyes searched his face, desperately seeking any hint that this wasn't real, that we could still find our way back to each other.

"Yes." By the scratchy timber of his voice, I could tell he was at his tipping point. "I can't repeat the past, Juli. We have to figure out what we want—and right now, it doesn't seem like you know."

His words were like ice water, chilling every hopeful thought I had clung to. I wanted to argue, to convince him that we weren't done. But the truth was, I didn't have the strength or clarity to fight him. Not when the shadows of my secrets loomed so large.

"Fine," I managed to whisper, my own voice about to crack.

"Good. If you'll excuse me," Chase huffed, his eyes flashing with determination, "I've got some leads to follow up on. I'm expecting you to keep your nose clean as well."

I had leads of my own to follow, but at the moment, all I could feel was the heavy void left behind as he walked out the door.

Twelve

I arrived at the fairgrounds with more *Butler's Pantry* goodies which I pulled along in my collapsable wagon. This time I'd included some breads and cookie mixes, ready to make in adorable mason jars with my signature "B" on the front label and all the organic ingredients on the back. A ruffled teal ribbon attached the cooking instructions. As for Chase, I understood to some degree our need for a break, but I didn't like it one bit.

Rather than toss and turn all night, I had thrown all my energy into cooking. With so many people stuck in town, I might as well give them something new and different from *The Butler's Pantry*. I even called Mark Walker, my manager, to see if we had enough staff to work at the café the remaining days of the fair. My gut told me I was missing out on some easy profits.

I rounded a corner near the saltwater taffy machines and saw Betty Henderson and Sandy Perkins. *Looks like someone's got their feathers ruffled already this morning*, I thought as I closed the gap. "Good morning, ladies!"

"Oh, thank goodness you're here." Sandy sighed and gave me a brief hug. "Betty and I are having a little disagreement. You need to tell us who's right."

"Oh boy, I don't want to be in the middle."

"Now, darlin', don't you worry. Sandy and I just think differently. Frankly, I see nothing to worry about, and she's in a tizzy because of her flawless reputation."

"Because it is flawless, Betty, and I plan to keep it that way." Sandy fluffed her platinum blonde bob, and I had to admit flawless was the perfect word for her. She's been openly supporting me since my return to New Hope and I loved that she had been good friends with my mom and that their rivalry was mostly for show.

"What exactly is going on?" I hated to ask. Sandy's flawlessness came with a price and that seemed to be stubbornness with a touch of bossy.

"I booked a celebrity chef to come and judge our wonderful pie contest. Sue Flaye from the *National Cooking Network*, have you seen her?" The pride and excitement in her voice were evident.

"Never seen her, but I know who she is." Oliver raved about her every chance he got. He even had a couple of her bestselling cookbooks. Based on things Oliver had told me, bringing Sue Flaye to New Hope was a major coup.

"Well," Sandy harrumphed, "our by-the-book sheriff won't let her enter."

"Oh boy."

"It's more than oh boy, it's a catastrophe!" She flung her arms into the air. "He told me she was not on the list, but my assistant this year—"

"That would be me," Betty announced, followed by a dramatic eye roll.

"Said she turned it in," Sandy finished, sending me a look that said she had her doubts about that.

"Which I did." Betty, in turn, shot me her *that woman is crazy* look, to which I returned my *I don't know what to do about it* face.

"He doesn't believe us, says he can't find the paperwork, and this is why I don't delegate. Do you understand where I'm coming from, Juli?" Sandy pleaded with me.

"I think so." I could tell this was the end of the world to Sandy, and I, for the life of me, couldn't figure out why Chase wasn't conceding to her request.

"I've tried to tell her we can find someone local," Betty reasoned, the sugary sweetness of southern hospitality coating every word, "someone who won't cost us a lot of money unlike that big-time celebrity."

"She would have been an amazing draw to the fair and our community. I don't know what I'm going to do." Sandy pinched the bridge of her nose as if she had a headache. I knew that feeling all too well when dealing with Sheriff Goody. "We have three days before the fair finale," Sandy pointed out and emphasized by holding up three fingers on her right hand. "We always have the pie contest to wrap up the fair. I'm beside myself!"

"Fire Chief Frank would certainly volunteer," Betty offered up.

"Frank Coleman loves food, Betty, he won't be an impartial judge at all. I'm sure his tastebuds are shot from all the hot wings he consumes now that his son owns the bar."

"Chase told me Frank recently put Riley in charge of the bar. I think that's great."

"Great for Riley, yes. Oh, that Frank would much rather spend his time at the firehouse tellin' stories to the young men and women on duty." Betty flicked her chunky wrist and grinned. "They are such a great family to our community. I keep tellin' our sweet April she needs to set her sights on someone like Riley Coleman. Maybe you can put in a good word, darlin'."

"Ladies, focus! What are we going to do about a judge?" Sandy wailed, then caught herself. "I mean, sorry Betty, but we need a judge."

"I think I might be able to help."

"Bless your heart!" Betty hugged me so tightly I almost couldn't breathe.

"He's a good friend of mine in Boston. I was just talking to him the other night, and he was thinking of coming to visit."

"If my celebrity can't get into this town, how are you going to get your friend in?" Betty sounded skeptical.

"Let me worry about that. I can handle the sheriff and his rule book." I left them both, confident of the challenge ahead as I continued on my way. Ollie would be more than happy to help, and I was sure I could bribe Gary with some of my cupcakes to help sneak him in. What the good sheriff didn't know wouldn't hurt him.

"Juuuliii," Squawked Scallywag as he flew overhead. "Trouble, Juli, trouble" He flapped his massive blue wings and settled on top of a trash can.

"How did you get out again? I'm going to buy you a new cage so you can't escape." I shook my fist at the peculiar parrot.

"EEEEKKKK!" he screamed, sounding almost human. Bystanders turned to stare at him.

"You crazy bird, go home!" I commanded and pointed in the direction of our houses.

"Watch out!" He tap-tap-tapped his beak on the top of the trash can. "Trouble coming." As quickly as he appeared, he shot into the air and flew away.

"That bird doesn't know what he's talking about," I mumbled as I changed direction toward the midway and tents. Only once again, I was proven wrong by that fowl fatale. There before me, talking to a seedy-looking carnival worker, was Eddie Costello, inky fedora and all. "I knew I didn't hallucinate you." And I wasn't about to let him out of my sight again.

"Eddie!" I called out as I came closer. The carnival worker gave him a pat on the shoulder, a nod in my direction and then disappeared between two tents.

Eddie's eyes raked over me, leaving a trail of discomfort in their wake. "Juli Butler," his voice dripped with false sweetness, making my skin crawl. "Fancy meeting you here."

"Is it?" I shot back, standing my ground. "I live here. You, on the other hand, certainly do not."

"It's a county fair. Last I knew, all were welcome. And considering there's been a murder and we're in lockdown, I have every right to be here." His chuckle was dark, as if he held a secret I wasn't privy to.

"What's so funny?" I demanded, my patience wearing thin.

"Here we are, together again. I've done nothing wrong, yet you somehow have it out for me. Am I right?" His grin was infuriatingly smug.

"I do have it out for you," I admitted, my voice steady. "I was suspicious of you from the first day you showed up at the gallery."

"Jealous is more like it," he sneered.

"Of you? Hardly." I narrowed my eyes. "I couldn't understand what hold you had over David and why you just suddenly appeared."

"The fact he never shared the information with you tells me he didn't trust you." His words struck a nerve, rekindling the doubts I had tried to bury. As memories of Boston flooded my mind, Eddie's words hit closer to home than I cared to admit. "By that look on your face, you're getting the real picture now, aren't you?"

"You're lying." I wanted to believe it was just another one of his manipulations.

"I brought a very lucrative business opportunity to his attention. Why wouldn't he share the details with his director and future wife?" His tone was almost mocking.

"Tell me why you're in New Hope," I pressed, refusing to let him rattle me further.

"It's personal, Juli." He stepped closer, his presence oppressive. "Now that I'm landlocked, I'd like to enjoy this down-home county fair. If you continue to harass me, I will report you to your boyfriend the sheriff, and you can share a cell with your ex-lover, David." He laughed. "Wouldn't that be an event to remember."

What was it with the boyfriend remarks?

"David's no longer in a cell, and you know nothing of my personal life. It's *me* who will report *you* for all the crimes you've committed."

"Is that so?" He took an ominous step toward me, but I stood my ground, even though my worry meter beat as fast as my heart.

"Yes, it is. You took a lot from me back in Boston. My future was there and somehow you weaseled your way into David's business."

"Did I step on your little toes?" he taunted, his voice dripping with mockery. "You took your fair share, so stop your crying."

"That event was my baby, my right of passage into the art world, and David let you run it. It was like I wasn't there at all." The pent-up anger and resentment I could never show in front of David spilled out.

"And, from what I heard, you were compensated quite well for your minimal efforts."

"What are you talking about? David didn't pay me at all, for *anything*!" I raised my voice, attracting the attention of several fair-goers who paused to stare. It had all been empty promises.

"Oh, he did, and don't think we don't know about it. You and your inventory rules. There's a record for everything in that gallery. He knows what you and your friends did. Why do you think he's here?"

"I know why he's here. The question is, why are you?"

"I have business to settle of my own. Let's just say Paul and Fawn are old friends of mine. It's a damn shame what happened to him."

"Did you have something to do with it?" My eyes widened in realization. "Oh my gosh, you set David up, didn't you?"

Eddie moved quickly, grabbing my arm and jerking me closer. "Watch what you say, Juli." The grit to his voice sent chills of doom across my body. "People are watching. It would be a damn shame if something happened to you, too."

"Juuuli! Juuuli!" I almost wilted to the ground at the sight of April running in our direction, holding the straps of her paisley backpack purse. "I'm so glad I found you."

"Remember what I said, Ms. Butler." Eddie tipped his inky fedora, smiled at April and followed the path his carnie friend had taken between the two tents.

"Hey, who was that?" April leaned around me to gaze down the narrow path, Eddie no longer in sight.

"Random fairgoer who sampled some items from my tent. He was trying to tell me the sesame peeps had too many sesame seeds." I closed my eyes and breathed through my nose to calm myself down.

"He was kind of creepy. You know you have to be careful being a woman alone out here, especially as it gets toward nighttime."

"You're right. Speaking of nighttime, sorry Chase and I lost you the other night."

"That's okay, I found some other friends to hang with. Oh, I got so distracted by your new friend I almost forgot why I was looking for you." April pulled off her purse and began sifting through it.

"Eddie is not my friend." Nor was he new, but I wasn't telling April that.

"Of course he is, or you wouldn't have used his name just now. See what I did there?" She dug deeper into the large pocket.

I wasn't following her at all. Without giving me details, Eddie had confirmed he had been up to something in Boston and roped David into it. But why hadn't David come clean?

"Ah! Here it is!" To my horror, April pulled out a small doll. The exact same voodoo doll both Rita and I had received.

I snatched it from her, fighting the urge to toss it into the nearest trash can. "Where did you get this!" I frantically studied it, turning it over in my hands for any indication of who might have made it or where it came from. There were no tags or identifiable markings other than being hand stitched. "Have you shown it to Chase? Did it have a note, or anything done to it?"

"I thought it looked like the one you found when someone broke into your house. I was kind of hoping maybe it was a secret admirer." She giggled and I inwardly groaned. To avoid a future misunderstanding, I bit back the words I really wanted to say.

"Was there a note? Where did you discover it?"

"No note or anything. I found it hanging in the darkroom of my studio. Scared the bajeepers out of me!" She placed a hand over her heart.

"Don't you think it's a voodoo doll? They seem so threatening. I got another one a couple days ago, and so did Rita."

"It's really not." April took it and brought it closer to her face. "I can see how you mixed it up with the rag dolls I'd made. Although I used my sewing machine, and these are clearly hand-stitched. I asked Aunt Betty about it because she knows all about the South."

Betty! Of course! Why hadn't I thought of that resource.

April continued, "She said that Voodoo, being something dark and scary, is what modern pop culture has led us to believe. Real Voodoo, spelled v-o-d-o-u, is a religion practiced in the Caribbean. They make dolls for healing and such, not for evil magic like we see in the movies. Aunt Betty is the one who said maybe I have a secret admirer like you did."

"Hey, you never know, right?" Only my secret admirer had an ulterior motive.

"I just hope it's not the same person. I really don't want to lose out to you, again." She sighed.

Normally, I would have taken advantage of that victory. Today, it felt ... different. Must be the rumor mill hadn't heard about our big break yet. I'm sure when they did, April would be the first one on the phone tree's call list and knocking on Chase's door. As much as I wanted to set things straight, there was still a mystery to solve. David may be home free, but a killer remained in New Hope. Thanks to Eddie, I had a sinking feeling the dolls and Paul's murder were somehow connected.

Which meant it wouldn't be long before Chase started finding my skeletons.

Thirteen

"How are you doing?" Rita asked me after Riley Coleman handed us our iced tea and summer salads. I'd chosen a strawberry, feta, and spinach salad while Rita ordered the chicken Caesar. "Are you guys really on a break?"

"I'm fine, I guess. He's right about one thing, this isn't new for us. We kind of have this push-pull effect on each other."

"I'm sure this case hasn't been easy for him. It's like the ghost of Christmas past came to haunt you, and Chase was in the way."

"Something like that." I stabbed a fork full of salad, not ready to discuss my feelings about the break. "Chase knew I was moving on the day I left for Boston. If he thought I wouldn't find someone else, well ... that's on him. I did love David, you know. Right up until—"

"That's okay," she reassured, "David does have that effect on people."

"Sorry." I put my fork down. "Are you guys together now?" The question seemed odd considering her fiancé had died only days ago. But given her behavior at the station, I had to wonder.

"There's no need to be sorry, Juli. And no, we're not together." She took a bite of her salad, and I watched her closely. She'd done a

125

complete turnaround in a twenty-four-hour period. She didn't appear to be a distraught fiancée and had returned to being the Rita Davis we all knew.

Kind of like nothing had ever happened.

"How are you?" I repeated her question.

"I'm okay. Now." She sipped her tea. "David has helped me a lot. Paul's reaction to the news about my divorce really hurt me. Come to find out he's no saint either."

"What do you mean?"

"He was involved with a woman he trained at the gym years ago. He groomed her for competition and traveled with her to different shows. I guess she was the one who convinced him to leave his sales job to become a fitness trainer and start his own gym. He took her advice, met Ivan and formed a business partnership. Then he and Fawn formed a partnership of their own."

"Did you say Fawn?" My radar beeped in rhythm with my quickening pulse.

"I know, different name, right?" Rita poured a packet of sugar into her tea.

"H-how long did you know about this?"

"He told me right away when we started getting serious. They'd been together for three years and then one day she just vanished."

"You mean, like, disappeared?"

Rita nodded. "He was devastated. They had talked about their future together, and he said she was all in. He thought something bad had happened to her until she reached out and said she couldn't handle the pressure anymore, and some guy named Eddie was helping her out of a jam."

"Wait, did you know all of this prior to Paul's murder?"

"Of course, he told me once we were seriously dating."

"Why didn't you say anything? They could have been additional suspects."

"Juli, I've never so much as seen a picture of them together. I have no clue what she looks like, nor do I care. She's an old flame and Paul pledged his love to me. We'd already been together for two years before he proposed. He'd had more than enough time to get over her or get back together with her. I'm sure she got wind of our engagement, and that's why she came sniffing back trying to get a job at their new gym."

"Rita!" I slapped my forehead. "Fawn is here, in New Hope?"

"I'm not sure on that one. But she's the manager Paul and Ivan were at odds over. I guess she was demanding a job."

"But you don't know if she's physically in town?" I pushed my salad aside and Rita shrugged. "Would Ivan know anything?"

"Maybe. Why is it so important to you? Especially now that David is cleared."

I smashed at the lemon wedge in my tea with the end of the straw. David being cleared was the main thing. Once Chase removed our lockdown status, he could leave to wherever he wanted, as long as it wasn't here. Now that Rita had mentioned Eddie and Fawn in the same sentence, there was validity to what Eddie had said at the fairgrounds. There was a story there and in order to get to the bottom of it, I was going to need help.

"Look, Juli," Rita continued when I failed to answer, "I appreciate you wanting to help with this investigation, but I really don't know anything else. Paul is dead, and I'm trying to move on. I'm sorry I kept this from you, but I honestly didn't see any connection."

"It's okay. After proving my own innocence during the Pete Seaver case, I'm sensitive to justice being served. There are a lot more people in town, which means we could have a lot of suspects to weed through."

"We? Does that mean Chase agreed to let you assist?"

"Not yet, but he will. I have some leads I'm going to follow up with him." I glanced down at my phone. "Which means I'd better get moving, don't want to be late."

"Of course, you go. Maybe while you're following up on those leads you can follow up on other things." She winked and I slipped off the high stool.

"Maybe."

My stomach was in knots at the thought of reaching out, as I texted Chase on my way home. He needed to know this information and I wanted him to understand I wasn't keeping things from him on purpose. Sharing details was manageable. But delving into those parts of myself that had learned some wild lessons, like loving someone who never quite lived up to my hopes no matter how much I tried—that was tough. And as much as I wanted to, discussing those feelings was challenging. Especially with Chase.

———

ONCE HOME, I SAT CROSS-LEGGED ON THE SOFA, running through the list of potential suspects, jotting notes and theories in my own notebook. My doorbell rang, and I heard a very familiar *woof.* I opened the door to Chase and Major, who bolted inside searching for his favorite toy. "C'mon in. He's looking for his bun-bun."

"Do I even want to know?"

"I bought him this un-stuffed rabbit. He treats it like it's a living animal, carrying it around all day. He even cries and fusses over it."

"Seriously?"

"It's adorable to watch." Major pranced into the living room with the bunny. He didn't fuss, or cry, or even bounce around the floor playing with it. "Huh. I bet it's because you're here."

"Sure." Chase held up a small envelope. "I found this taped to my front door. Care to talk about it?"

"I know." I couldn't meet his eyes. "I was clearing out the back room and there it was, hanging from that same piece of twine on a hook by the back door. I thought you might want it back."

"Does this have anything to do with me saying we needed a break?"

"Of course not," I replied, not completely sure.

He sighed heavily. "I gave that key to you. I wanted you to have it then and I want you to have it now. In case of storms, power outages, or just—"

"I'm not that young girl anymore, Chase. I can handle any storm."

"I know. Just do me a favor and keep it." He leaned around me to set it on the vintage wooden trunk with embossed leather accents I'd repurposed into a coffee table. Another great find from Mom's antique store. He straightened up and slid his hands in the pockets of his jeans. "I got your text."

"Yes! Right!" I dropped onto the sofa and grabbed my notebook. "I know you don't want me involved in the case, but I did look into some theories I have, and actually, Rita gave me some important information this afternoon over lunch."

"What do you have?" He took the cushion next to me and pulled out his own notebook.

"Who bonked you on the head?" I eyed him suspiciously.

"What do you mean?"

"I thought you'd have a problem with me getting information."

"It's your *methods* I have a problem with. Jogging at night, sneaking into the O'Toole's house and escaping out a window with a rope, shall I go on?"

"Point taken. That was only to clear my own name and get you to believe me."

"If you say so. I gotta admit, you do have darn good theories." Chase grinned and my heart tripped a beat. He must have seen my building excitement because he quickly added, "Don't even think it, we're not partners or consulting or anything else in this case."

"Whatever." I leaned back against the cushion, feeling comfortable with our vibe. We may be on a break, but we could still talk to each other and be comfortable and that was important. "From my conversation with Rita, I'm getting the impression that Ivan Petrov could be a person of interest."

"Gary has already questioned him. He checks out clear."

"He had a disagreement with Paul, over a couple things actually."

"Like what? Gary said Ivan voiced concerns about the new gym opening and all the legalities now that Paul was dead. Gary is pretty intuitive, if he suspected any tension with Ivan, he would have mentioned it."

"According to Rita, Paul had an ex-lover—"

"This is becoming a recurring theme, isn't it. First Rita, then you and now Paul?"

"Ouch. Not necessary, Sheriff." I scowled. I suppose I had it coming, so I recapped just to make my own mark. "So ... his *ex-lover* came back to town and demanded Paul make her a manager at the new gym. Ivan was against it and let's not forget what I overheard with Ivan and those T-Factor Supplements people."

"Right." Chase scanned his notebook. "Ivan wanted the deal with the Tullersons and Paul did not."

"I think there was a lot of tension between them about this whole gym expansion and the direction they were going. Ivan even told me he wants to stay small and more specialized so they can charge more."

He tapped his pen on his knee. "You think he's dissolving everything related to the expansion now that Paul is dead?"

"Seems that way to me. Remember, the Tullersons were mad at Paul because he backed out of the deal in the first place."

"You really think Ivan or the Tullersons killed Paul?"

"I think both parties had motive, for sure. But there's one other thing." I gnawed at my lower lip, realizing it was now or never.

"What's that?"

"Eddie Costello."

"The drug dealer from the gallery?" Chase studied me, his face filled with suspicion.

"Yes. Well, the last time I saw him he was at the gallery."

Chase ran a hand over his face. "Why are you telling me this now?"

"I wasn't sure if there was anything to tell, but then I ran into him at the fairgrounds. I know he's trying to scare me by making threats and mentioning David and the gallery."

"Wait, the man threatened you?"

"It's fine. He doesn't scare me." I kept my bravado up, still not ready to admit my Boston faults. "He mentioned how Paul and Fawn were old friends of his. I thought he was bluffing, but then Rita said Paul had a prior relationship with Fawn, confirming what Eddie had said." I paused a beat to make sure Chase was keeping up. "They had a professional and personal relationship and then she suddenly disappeared. Paul didn't know where she was until months later when she reached out and told him Eddie helped her out of a jam. She stayed away, and he thought they were over. That's when he met Rita."

Chase nodded, looking pensive. "Only this Fawn woman didn't think they were over."

"Bingo! Now she's in New Hope and so is Eddie. I don't know what that means or how it fits into Paul's murder, but it's too coincidental."

"That's a lot of information." Chase scribbled more into his notebook. When he looked up, his eyes bore into mine, reading me like an open book. "What have you gotten yourself into? Julianna, I need to know right now."

"I'm not sure, but I think it might have something to do with my Oscar Royce painting."

"The one you're having Rita copy in stained glass?"

I nodded again, watching his features morph from questioning to anger. "Chase, I never thought the painting would be an issue. I took it the night before I left town. David owed me and my friends money, and he wasn't paying. I had a feeling I was being set up to take the fall for the drug smuggling, so we all decided to take what was owed us from the inventory."

"You stole the painting."

"I prefer *collecting payment*."

"I knew you were bringing trouble to town, Julianna!" He rose from the couch, clenching his fists. "If this man, Eddie, is after your painting. He's probably the one sending the voodoo dolls. Did you know April got one too? How the hell did you get her involved in this?"

"I didn't get her involved. If you must know, she checked with Betty, and they are not voodoo dolls. They are just dolls with messages. April's doll didn't happen to say anything, so she thinks she had a secret admirer."

"Not funny, Juli."

"I'm not trying to be funny. I'm trying to help you with the suspects."

"I think you've done enough. I've got my notes. Gary and I will investigate. Your job is done, is that understood?"

"Sure."

He whistled for Major, who dropped his bunny and followed him to the door. He started down the steps and turned around. When our eyes met, he seemed sad, and I felt a surge of fear about where our relationship was headed. Speaking my truth had turned out exactly as I'd feared.

"We'll be okay," he said and all I could do was nod, even though in that moment, I didn't believe him.

Fourteen

I drummed my fingers against the windowsill, my eyes darting between the grandfather clock's solemn face and the empty driveway outside. The rhythmic ticking of the clock seemed to mock my growing anxiety as I awaited Oliver's arrival.

"Come on, Oliver," I muttered, pulling my phone out of the back pocket of my jeans. "Where are you?" I texted my question.

As if on cue, the crunch of gravel under tires caught my attention. A mix of relief and excitement washed over me. Sliding the phone back into my pocket, I hurried to the front door ready to welcome one of my best friends.

Only the scene unfolding in the early morning light was far from the warm reunion I'd anticipated.

Two figures tumbled onto the front lawn, a tangle of limbs and raised voices. My eyes widened in shock when I recognized Chase's broad shoulders and the glint of his sheriff's badge. He was straddling a man—Oliver—pinning him to the ground with surprising force.

"What in the world?" I gasped, my voice not quite a whisper.

I watched, frozen in place, as Chase's face contorted with anger, his usual calm demeanor shattered. "You think you can just waltz in here and stir up trouble?" he growled, his grip on Oliver's shirt tightening.

Oliver, despite his compromised position, managed a wry chuckle. "Is this how New Hope welcomes all its guests, Sheriff? I must say, it's quite the reception."

My mind raced, torn between confusion and concern. What could have possibly transpired in the few minutes since Oliver's arrival to provoke such a reaction from Chase?

"Stop it!" I finally cried out while marching down the front steps. "Chase, what are you doing?"

Both men's heads snapped towards me, surprise evident in their expressions. I froze, still several steps away, my hands trembling slightly as I remembered myself in a similar situation not too long ago.

"Juli," Chase started, his voice softer but still laced with tension. "This isn't what it looks like. I can explain—"

"Then start explaining," I interrupted, my eyes darting between Chase and Oliver. "Because from where I'm standing, it looks like you're assaulting my best friend on *my* front lawn."

Oliver coughed, attempting to sit up despite Chase's weight still pressing him down. "That would indeed be me, Sheriff. Oliver Thompson, owner and head chef of *Savory Elegance Catering*, Boston. Jules, I'm touched by the small-town welcome wagon. Though I must admit, I'd prefer a less physical form of endearment. A bottle of pinot noir would have sufficed."

Tension hardened Chase's features, his eyes flashing with barely contained fury. "Sorry, not buying it, buddy. This town has been on lockdown, nobody in and nobody out. Where have you been hiding? You're certainly not here just for the pie contest."

"Actually, he is." I leveled him with a stern glare, frustration building within. "I invited Oliver here myself, at the request of Sandy—"

"So, you bypassed my authority. *Again,*" Chase cut in, finally releasing his hold on Oliver and standing up.

Oliver dusted himself off, his usual charm slightly dampened by the scuffle. "I do love a good pie." His statement was barely heard as Chase and I faced off.

"You may have invited him, but how did he get through the roadblocks?"

I took a moment to compose myself, knowing by coming clean I was implicating someone else. "Gary helped me and gave Oliver's name to the officers posted at the blocks."

Chase stood with his shoulders squared and feet firmly planted, a stance that spoke of his determination and simmering anger. His eyes bore into mine with an intensity that was hard to ignore. His hands were fisted tight as his sides, as if he was trying to keep a lid on his emotions. "I'm getting a little tired of people going behind my back."

My heart sank, and a heaviness settled in my chest. "If you loosened up a little, we wouldn't have to. Remember, it's okay to toss out the rule book." I closed my eyes for a moment, taking a deep breath. When I opened them, my gaze was steady and filled with resolve. "All right, both of you, inside. Now. We don't need to give the neighborhood anything else to talk about."

As I ushered them towards the house, my thoughts became a tangled web of uncertainties. The case that had seemed straightforward was now a labyrinth of possibilities, each turn revealing new questions. I glanced at Chase, his stern profile igniting a flutter in my chest that I quickly suppressed.

"All right," I said, my voice steadier than I felt as I stood before Chase in my cozy country kitchen. "I'm sure you remember the last time something like this happened, I was on the receiving end of the lecture. Let's see how you like it, Lawman."

Oliver rested his elbows on the counter, fully invested in the drama about to unfold. "Jules, it's a little early for popcorn, but I do see a full pot of coffee. Mind if I pour?"

"I'll take one, too, please. Chase?"

"Sure," Chase replied, his green eyes sharp. "It was a case of mistaken identity, nothing more. I just came off night-watch at the fairgrounds and thought he was breaking in. I thought he was Eddie."

I felt a pang of exasperation. "You are a respected member of this community. You can't just go around tackling people."

"In all fairness, you were one hundred percent justified, and it was a clean hit," Oliver stated as he handed Chase a steaming mug of coffee.

"Appreciate that." Chase raised the mug in salute and Oliver returned the gesture. "Also appreciate the coffee. I'm taking this back to my place and catching up on some sleep. Oliver, great to meet you. I'm sure I'll see you around. Hope I didn't hurt you."

"Likewise, Sheriff, and ... no harm, no foul." Oliver shook his hand and walked over to the coffee pot to top off his mug.

Chase stopped beside me. "What about you. You good?" He tapped his mug against mine.

"For now," I grumbled, squinting as I tried to process what had just happened. I shook my head in disbelief, my lips pressing into a thin line. "I can't believe you jumped him like a schoolyard bully."

Oliver's voice cut through our awkward silence. "Hey, it's all good!"

Chase walked out without another word and my thoughts drifted. Could I trust my own judgment? This case, Chase, Eddie —everything seemed to be slipping through my fingers like sand. I'd returned to New Hope seeking simplicity, yet here I was, at the center of a mystery yet again, one that threatened to unravel the very fabric of my peaceful life.

Oliver's voice broke through my reverie. "Juli, I know this is overwhelming, but you're more capable than you realize. You have a knack for uncovering truths, even when they're buried deep."

I met his gaze across the center island in my kitchen, grateful for his faith in me. "But what if I'm wrong? What if I can't solve this?"

"You won't be alone," he assured me, a knowing smile playing on his lips. He glanced pointedly in the direction Chase had taken. "You have allies here, Juli. People who care about you and want to help. Perhaps it's time to let them in, especially those closest to your heart."

I felt my cheeks warm, at the thought of Chase. "Ollie, I don't think now is the time—"

"On the contrary," Oliver interrupted gently. "Now might be the perfect time. Life's too short for unspoken truths. Trust me on that."

As I pondered Oliver's words, I couldn't help but feel a glimmer of hope amidst the chaos. Perhaps facing the truth—both in the case and in my heart—was the key to finding my way forward.

I grasped Oliver's hands, my voice thick with emotion as the late afternoon light streamed through the windows in *Petite Four Paws Café*. "Oliver, I can't thank you enough for coming. The pie contest is the finale of the fair and means so much to New Hope. Having you here as our top judge, it's just ... it's everything."

Oliver squeezed my hands gently. "Jules, I wouldn't have missed it for the world. You know I'd do anything for you. I'm proud of you for starting your own business here." His appreciative gaze scanned the room, taking in the paw-print boarder, black and brown accents and glass jars containing treats for everyone's pets. "This place is amazing, and it suits you. Chardonnay would give you a five-star meow."

I managed a wavering smile. "Your support means more than you know, especially now. Everything feels so ... uncertain."

As Oliver excused himself to freshen up, my smile faded. The weight of recent events pressed down on my shoulders, and I wrapped my arms around myself, as if trying to hold all the pieces together.

"What have I gotten myself into?" I whispered, standing in front of the large picture window of the café, gazing at locals and visitors enjoying what our small town had to offer. Images flashed through my mind: the scuffle outside, Chase's intense gaze, the mysterious notes. Each memory sent a chill down my spine.

I absently circled my finger around the rim of my glass of iced tea. "If someone's really coming after me … after the people I care about …" I couldn't finish the thought, and my throat tightened with fear. I took a deep breath, trying to center myself. "I need to be careful," I murmured. "One wrong move and …" I shook my head, pushing away the dark thoughts, but the nagging fear remained, a constant reminder as I contemplated my next steps.

Oliver's footsteps echoed as he returned, his brow furrowed with concern. He placed a gentle hand on my shoulder. "Jules," he said, his voice soft but firm. "I can see the wheels turning in that brilliant mind of yours. But there's something we need to discuss."

"What?"

"It's about Chase," Oliver began, a knowing smile playing at the corners of his mouth. "I've grown to be a great judge of character since starting the catering company. I've become very good at reading a room, and let me tell you, I've never seen a man look at anyone the way Chase looks at you."

My heart sank a little. Ollie meant well but he didn't know all our history. There was so much more to think about than my relationship with Chase. I feared we'd finally reached an impasse, and I needed to move past it. "Ollie, I—"

"Hold on," he interrupted, holding up a hand. "I know it's complicated, what with the investigation and all. But take it from someone who knows—life's too short to let something special slip away."

I bit my lip, my gaze dropping to the floor. I felt like Chase and

I had been up and down this road too many times. Could Oliver be right? "But what if—"

"No 'what ifs,'" Oliver insisted. "Talk to him, Juli. I can tell Chase is a good man with a good heart. If he wasn't, you would never have a history with him. Don't let your connection go to waste because of fear or doubt."

As Oliver's words sank in, I felt a maelstrom of emotions threatening to overwhelm me. I turned toward the window, my reflection a blur of uncertainty. "I want to," I whispered, my voice barely audible. "But it's not that easy. There's so much at stake. The case, the café, my heart ..."

My throat tightened against the sob I refused to release. Memories of tender moments with Chase intermingled with the weight of the investigation. The pressure seemed to build inside my chest, making it hard to breathe.

"What if I'm not strong enough?" I asked more to myself than Oliver. "What if I can't solve this mystery and keep everyone safe? What if I've already let Chase down?" My hands trembled slightly as I gripped the cold glass of tea, anchoring myself against the tide of doubt threatening to pull me under.

I took a deep breath, my fingers uncurling from the tall glass. I turned to face Oliver, a newfound resolve settling in my eyes. "You're right," I said, my voice steadier now. "I can't keep running from this."

Oliver's face lit up with a warm smile. "That's the Jules we all know and love! Now, don't you worry about me. I'm sure Sandy can show me around while you go find your sheriff."

I nodded, grabbing my purse. "Thank you, Ollie. You have no idea how happy I am that you're here."

I waved goodbye to Mark Walker, my shop manager, who had agreed to close up since Andie and Scott were still at *The Butler's Pantry* tent at the fair. As I stepped out into the warm summer air, my heart raced with anticipation. The fairgrounds weren't far, and

I could already hear the distant hum of music and laughter. With each step, my determination grew.

Fifteen

The Lewis County Fair sprawled before me, a kaleidoscope of colors and activity. I weaved through the crowd, my senses overwhelmed by the scent of funnel cakes and the cheerful shouts from the game booths.

"Okay, Juli," I muttered to myself, scanning the sea of faces. "Where would Chase be?" I passed the livestock exhibition, usually a favorite of his, but no sign of the sheriff. The Ferris wheel loomed overhead, and I paused, my eyes sweeping the queue. "Come on, Chase." My fingers fidgeted with the strap of my purse. "Where are you?"

A group of laughing teenagers jostled past, momentarily throwing me off balance. I steadied myself against a nearby booth, my heart pounding not just from the near fall but from the gravity of what I was about to do.

What am I even going to say to him? I wondered, biting my lower lip. The weight of unspoken words and stolen glances hung heavily in my mind. But Oliver's advice echoed in my ears, spurring me forward. I pressed on, my eyes darting from face to face in the bustling crowd. The mid-afternoon sun beat down, and I felt a bead of sweat forming on my brow—from the heat or nerves, I couldn't tell. The fairgrounds seemed to stretch endlessly before me, a maze of attractions and possibilities. And somewhere in that maze was Chase, and the chance to finally confront the elephant in the room.

The break wasn't working. I missed us. I missed *him*.

As I rounded the corner of the Ferris wheel, I nearly collided with a solid form. Strong hands steadied me, and I looked up to find Chase's concerned eyes searching my face.

"Juli," he said, his voice low and urgent. "I've been looking for you. We need to have a conversation about—"

A commotion near the ring toss booth cut him off. My breath caught as I spotted Eddie, our prime suspect, shoving his way through the crowd. I didn't want him to see me and think I was on to him. I needed to formulate a plan with Chase. I decided to take a leap of faith that Chase would play along. Spinning in Chase's arms, I pressed my lips on his, thankful his body blocked Eddie's view.

The contact was electric.

For a moment, Chase tensed in surprise, but then wrapped his arms around me and deepened the kiss. My heart raced, and I couldn't tell if it was from the thrill of our ruse or the unexpected passion behind Chase's response.

When we finally broke apart, I peeked over Chase's shoulder. Eddie had disappeared into the crowd. I let out a shaky breath, both relieved and oddly disappointed that the moment was over.

"Well," Chase said, his voice husky. "That was ... unexpected."

I stepped back, smoothing my hair and trying to regain my composure. "Sorry, I saw Eddie and panicked. I didn't want him to think we were onto him. We need a plan."

Chase appeared as out of sorts as I was from our kiss. "Eddie?" His eyes remained intense as they searched the immediate vicinity. "Quick thinking. But Juli, we really do need to address things."

The cacophony of the fair faded to a dull roar as my heart thundered in my chest. Chase's eyes softened with an emotion I couldn't quite place. I took a deep breath, preparing myself for what was to come, suddenly unsure of what to do with my hands.

"Chase," I began, my voice trembling slightly. "I ... I couldn't agree more."

He nodded, his expression blended curiosity with concern. My stomach twisted with nerves. But I pressed on, my words careful and earnest. "I can't keep pretending there isn't something here," I said, gesturing between us. "This attraction, this tension—it's affecting everything, including the case. This break isn't working, and I think ... I think we owe it to ourselves to address it."

Chase's eyes widened, a flicker of surprise and hope crossing his features before he quickly composed himself. He ran a hand through his hair, a gesture I recognized as a sign of his own nervousness.

His voice was low and hesitant. "I've been feeling it, too, since the moment you came back to town. After everything that's happened, I don't feel it's the right time to skew our focus."

"I know. It's pretty complicated, isn't it?"

Chase took a step closer, his eyes insightful as they searched my face. "When have we been anything *but* complicated, Scarlett? All the more reason to slow things down and talk about it. That is, when you're ready. Instead of a break, maybe we call it more of an intermission."

"An intermission," I mused, my voice barely audible above the carnival noise. "That's what we're calling it?"

Chase's eyes softened as he looked at me with a nod. "Yeah, it feels right. We both know there's still something here. We just need time to figure it out."

I nodded in agreement. "Why don't we start by finding Eddie and getting some answers."

"Only one problem, Scarlett, I don't know what he looks like."

I slipped my hand into his and started walking. "Stocky like a bouncer trying to be a mobster. He's most likely the only guy wearing an inky black fedora."

"Roger that."

As we weaved through the crowd, my mind whirled. I never expected my peaceful existence in New Hope to be turned upside down for a second time. I'd left the city to escape chaos and tension, yet here I was, now on a mission to track down a potential criminal at the county fair.

Suddenly, Chase grabbed my arm. "There," he whispered, nodding towards a shadowy figure near the Ferris wheel. My breath caught as I confirmed Eddie's silhouette. We approached cautiously, but Eddie spotted us and sneered.

"Well, well. If it isn't the Boston burnout and her hillbilly boyfriend," Eddie spat.

I stepped forward, my voice steady despite my spiked adrenaline. "Eddie, we just want to talk. New Hope isn't your kind of place. What are you really doing here?"

Eddie's face contorted with rage. He lunged forward, yanking my wrist. "Listen, you little—"

Before he could finish, Chase's fist connected with Eddie's jaw. In a blur of motion, Chase had Eddie on the ground, handcuffs clicking into place. "You okay?" He asked over his shoulder, concern etched on his face.

"I'm fine. Let's get him talking."

Eddie glared at us. "I don't have to tell you anything."

Chase tightened the cuffs then hauled him to his feet. "You've got two options. Start talking or spend the night in jail."

Eddie's bravado crumbled. "Fine! I could care less about Rivera; we had our fun back in the day. I followed Fawn here. She showed up on my doorstep years ago. Couldn't handle the pressure of the circuit or her relationship with Rivera. Somehow, she thought she could use those steroids at the gym and not fall back into old habits, ya know? Once a junkie, always a junkie. She convinced me to hook her up just to take the edge off."

"Then what is she doing back here?" I asked, not making sense of their relationship.

"Once she settled in, I thought she was in control, so I left her alone while I was out of town working for David. Come to find out, she'd hooked up with one of my buddies to get what she really needed."

"Technically, you were working for me, not David," I corrected, unable to hide my displeasure.

"Whatever helps you sleep at night, cupcake."

"Watch it, Costello," Chase growled.

"You should really lighten up," Eddie said to Chase. "My beef's not with you."

"Again, why are you in New Hope?" I stepped closer and received a warning look from Chase. He didn't realize I'd dealt with Eddie before. I wasn't afraid.

"I'm here to haul her fanny back to Chicago. I paid her debt to my buddy. She's going to work off what she owes me, and then I'm through with her."

My mind reeled. Fawn, involved in drugs? It seemed impossible, yet it explained so much.

Eddie continued, his voice bitter. "She was obsessed with Rivera even before she contacted me. She found out he was getting married and snapped. She was determined to convince Paul to take her back, work with him at the gym, and get her fix like before. But now she's gone underground. I can't find her anywhere."

The muscles in Chase's jaw tightened. "Eddie Costello, you're under arrest for—"

"For what?" Eddie sneered. "I've got nothing on me. No drugs, no weapons. You got *nothing*."

I watched helplessly as Chase reluctantly removed the handcuffs. Eddie rubbed his wrists, shooting us a triumphant look before disappearing into the crowd, no doubt searching for Fawn.

As the Ferris wheel creaked above us, I turned to Chase feeling utterly lost. "Now what?"

Chase sighed, raking his fingers through his hair. "I don't

know. We're back to square one, with no suspect and now, no leads on Fawn."

I stared at the spot where Eddie had vanished, the cheerful music of the fair suddenly feeling out of place. More skeletons than necessary had followed me to New Hope. As I stood there with Chase, I couldn't shake the feeling that this investigation was far from over, and dangers still lurked in the shadows of New Hope.

Sixteen

The aroma of freshly brewed coffee mingled with the scent of cinnamon rolls as I leaned against the polished counter at *Ringo's*, warm light streamed through the windows casting a flash onto all the chrome details. A heavy sigh escaped me as I shared a frustrated glance with Chase and Gary.

"So, we've hit the reset button," I said, my voice tinged with disappointment. "David von Hoffster was cleared by Rita, Ivan Petrov's story checks out ... even the Tullersons are merely marketing their supplements off the grid."

Chase nodded, his posture reflecting my emotions. "I know it's not what we hoped for, but we can't ignore the facts. Ivan may be abrasive, but he and Paul were business partners. He didn't kill him. He even volunteered for a polygraph." It was his turn to sigh next as he wiped the weariness from his face. "I've got Mayor Montgomery wanting a status report every day, morning and night. This lockdown is causing us to lose revenue. I need something solid that will get her off my back for a while."

My mind tracked like a complex puzzle, trying to assemble all the colorful pieces. "There must be something we're missing. Some connection we haven't made yet."

The bell above the door chimed, and April rushed in, her face etched with concern. "Chase! Thank goodness I've caught up with you." He began to rise off the stool, but she wrapped her arms around his shoulders, forcing him back down with her head nestled under his chin. "I heard you and Juli had a break." She straightened, placing her hand on her chest as if to catch her breath, and stared curiously at me before turning her attention back to him. Her hand caressed his cheek when she said in a sugary-sweet voice, "Are you okay?"

Before I could set her straight, Chase's calm voice cut through the tension. "I'm fine, April. There wasn't a break—we're still working on it. You know, like an intermission before the next act." He shot a quick glance in my direction and his crooked smile caused warmth to bloom in my chest at his gentle reassurance.

He's always so patient, even when everyone around him is on edge.

"Oh." April flushed with embarrassment. "I'm so sorry. I feel like such a fool."

"It's okay. Easy misunderstanding. I appreciate your concern."

"Always, Chase. You know that." Chase nodded, and I silently counted to five before she took the hint. "You all enjoy breakfast. I'll catch up to you later." As she turned to leave, she pressed a button on her phone and raised it to her ear. All I heard was, "You were wrong!" She shot through the door at the same time Sam was coming in, his eyes wide with excitement.

"We got a hit!" Sam exclaimed, brandishing a file. "Fingerprints from the insulin pen."

"Excellent!" Gary cried out as Sam rushed over.

"Who's the lucky match? Anyone local?" Chase questioned.

Sam hopped upon the stool on the other side of Chase. "Not local as far as I can tell, but they are here since you still have us on lockdown. The prints are a direct match to a Ms. Fawnella Jane Wilson!"

The energy in the room shifted instantly. I straightened,

setting my cup on the counter with a little too much force. "Fawnella? Paul's ex-girlfriend?"

Gary's expression became pensive. "If she's our suspect, where would she hide?" Chase started to speak, but Gary cut him off while he worked through the theory. "In plain sight," he finished, snapping his fingers. "The fairgrounds! Easy to blend in during the day, plenty of places to hide at night."

I slapped my hand on the table in agreement with Gary. "The fairgrounds. Of course. It's the perfect cover!"

"Let's move," Chase commanded, already heading for the door. "We'll split up when we get there. Juli, you're with me."

As we rushed out of *Ringo's*, I couldn't shake the feeling that we were on the precipice of something big. *We're coming for you, Fawnella.*

———

THE FAIRGROUNDS BUZZED WITH ACTIVITY AS THE FINAL day drew near. The scent of funnel cakes and grilled corn filled the air, a stark contrast to the tension I felt coiling around the worry meter in my stomach. Chase and I weaved through the crowds, scanning for anything or anyone out of the ordinary.

"Juli! Chase!" A familiar voice called out. We turned around to find Oliver waving at us from behind a cotton candy stand, looking slightly frazzled.

"Oliver?" I raised an eyebrow. "What are you doing hiding back there?"

He grinned sheepishly. "Trying to avoid the pie contest bakers. Sandy introduced me, and some were exceptionally chatty. I take my duty very seriously and must remain impartial. No contact until after the final judging. But the best part? Oh my, I can barely contain myself!"

"Oliver, I haven't seen you this excited since you had a one-on-one session with Gordon Ramsey."

"I know, right? Well, I just had the most marvelous Zoom call with *Sue Flaye*! And Sandy Perkins? She's a gem, I absolutely love her. Would you believe I have both Sue and Sandy on my speed dial now? Oh, and Betty Henderson invited me to church on Sunday!"

I couldn't help but smile at his enthusiasm. "Sounds like you're settling in nicely. They'll probably adopt you next."

"Or set you up with April," Chase added with a chuckle.

I shot him a stunned look. While I always thought April would make a great wife, Oliver was like my brother and bestie rolled into one. I would not want April as my sister-in-law. "Chase ..." My warning tone didn't even compare to his.

"Oh no, here come some other bakers, help me hide!" Oliver resumed his spot behind the cotton candy.

"Be nice to April," he reminded me as our eyes met. "You know," he added softly, "I'm grateful you had such a loyal friend back in Boston. Oliver's a great guy."

"Just wait till you meet the others," I replied, my voice thick with emotion. I missed them all very much. I quickly pulled myself together as David, Rita and Gary approached, their faces covered in frustration.

"Any luck?" Chase asked, his sheriff's instincts kicking in.

"Nothing. Seriously, Boss, we don't even have a description of the suspect." Gary tossed his hands in the air. "Rita never met or saw pictures of her and Ivan was no help at all. He claimed he met her once, but he was on the phone making a deal so he didn't pay attention. He said she was short, whatever that means. I wish we had some drones or something."

David pulled out his phone, revealing a photo. "Maybe this will help. Eddie sent it. It's Fawn—petite, tan skin, long curly blonde hair."

I couldn't resist a jab. "Eddie, huh? David, you told me you didn't know where he was? And how long have you had this?" I grabbed his phone and quickly sent the image to myself. "I can't believe you."

"And I can't believe you," he said as he snatched his phone back while I sent the image from my phone to everyone else. "He literally just sent it, darling, so take a breath, okay?"

"Nice job, Juli," Chase complimented in true sheriff style. "Team, everyone take a look at our suspect. Fawnella Jane Wilson." He opened his messages to view the photo. "Anyone have questions?"

I stared at the picture then looked up as a flash of blonde caught my eye. "There!" I shouted, pointing towards the hall of mirrors. We all took off running.

"Gary, you and your group cover the exit. We'll go in." Chase flagged them toward the other end of the portable trailer-like building full of mirrors. As we entered the disorienting maze of reflections, Fawn seemed to vanish into thin air. Chase broke off left, leaving me with Oliver to go right.

As we navigated the twisting corridors, Oliver kept pausing, his gaze fixed on something I couldn't see. "What are you doing?" I asked as he stared at an empty mirror with a goofy smile on his face.

"There's a woman," he murmured. "Brown hair, the most beautiful smile I've ever seen. She keeps waving at me."

I rolled my eyes. "Oliver, focus! We're looking for Fawn, remember? Blonde hair, blonde hair!"

But Oliver seemed entranced, smiling and waving at empty air. "What if I never see her again?"

My annoyance increased as we reached the exit, empty-handed.

"We were so close," I groaned and leaned against a signpost, my heart sinking. "There's so much ground to cover. We have to find her before nightfall when she goes into hiding."

"Here she comes! Get ready!" I heard Chase call from inside, followed by a high-pitched scream.

"We're ready!" I waved Oliver to stand next to me at the base of the exit steps, arms ready to make the grab.

"Get her!" Chase yelled.

A small blonde girl bolted from the hall of mirrors, screaming as if Satan were on her tail. I reached out to grab her when a firm arm reached in front of me, I was immediately hip-checked, and then someone snatched the girl.

"Excuse me! That's my daughter." The woman scowled and pulled her daughter, probably all of seven—a very tall seven—out of my reach.

Chase came flying out next, breathless, and looking at our empty arms in confusion. That is until the mother, still holding her daughter, stepped in front of him.

"Sheriff Hargrave, what is going on here? My Katie is scared half to death."

"Wait, you mean she was in there? I thought I was chasing our suspect. Mrs. Parker, I'm terribly sorry."

"You should be! I will be letting the mayor know you have a nasty habit of frightening small children."

"Mrs. Parker, please, that's not necessary. Please accept my apology. We're on the lookout for a small woman, she entered the hall of mirrors. Somehow, I must have seen Katie pass by in the mirror and thought it was her."

"I saw her," Katie offered up. "She was right by me most of the time."

"On purpose," I deduced. "She's clever, Chase. We need to stay on our toes."

"Excuse me, Katie," Oliver asked, "but did you happen to see another lady in there? She had brown hair ..."

"Oliver! Really?" I scolded him as Mrs. Parker spun around and marched away with Katie in tow.

"What? I need to know if I imagined her. She was ... magnifique," he added the French accent and pinched his fingers to his lips in a kiss.

"You'll live, I promise."

A flash of blue passed through a ray of sunshine. "Trouuuuble, Juuuli!"

The minute I stepped forward I caught a glimpse of someone curled up against a mirror, trying to stay out of sight. I stepped away, pretending I was getting a better look at Scallywag as he did another fly by.

"Woof-Woof-Woof!"

"Major?" Chase turned in time to catch the giant fluff ball as he launched over the exit steps. "Whoa, buddy!" Chase lost his balance a little but remained upright. Major's paws hit the ground, and he stared at the exit, emitting a low, rumbling growl.

"She's in there," I whispered to Chase.

Chase clicked his tongue, and the dog made eye contact. Chase gave the next command with the subtle shift of his head, and Major crept closer. When he froze, Chase gave me the hand signal to stay put, while he moved in behind his dog.

"Leave me alone!" Fawn was a blur of movement as she fled the building and sprinted out into the crowd. An amber medicine bottle rolled toward Chase's feet.

"What is it?" I asked, stepping closer.

"Oxy. And by the number of pills left in this bottle, it's safe to say she's under the influence. Be careful, team."

I couldn't help myself, "I kind of like partner better."

"No." He whistled to Major who impressively did not pursue Fawn. All it took was a whistle from Chase and the dog was a streak of fluff bolting through the crowd. "He'll catch up to her, c'mon."

We jogged after the dog, with the bird high in the sky catching an updraft. I had to admit, his blue and gold giant wingspan looked majestic as he soared. "Major was pretty impressive back there. What happened to the lazy furball?"

"I've been working with him on my off days. He's not a German Shepard or a Malinois, but he likes the structure of the lessons and he's not destroying the house when I need to work late."

"Then Lily was right." I smiled, reminding him of the vet's suggestion, and proud of Chase for actually listening.

"Yes, Lily was right." He confirmed with a knowing smile of his own.

We jogged out past the vendor tents and the Grand Stage to where a large glass holding tank had been set up for the log rolling competition. Inside it was a giant log with a solid platform on each end. There, getting ready to step off the platform and onto the log, was Fawn. We could hear Major's growl as he stalked her like a shaggy lion.

Seventeen

"**I**mpressive," I panted between breaths of air.

"How's that nighttime jogging working out for you?" Chase teased as he was only slightly out of breath. I could only shake my head. Full sentences would take too much effort.

"We've got to stop her," Gary said as he approached, barely winded. "I'll sneak around and move toward the log from the other side.

The log roll platform groaned ominously beneath the weight as Major cornered Fawn. Her petite frame taut, like a bowstring drawn to its limit, ready to snap at any moment. My heart pounded as I watched the standoff unfold.

Gary's voice cut through the tense silence. "I'll cut her off."

Before anyone could react, Fawn darted across the log with surprising agility, her feet finding purchase on the slick surface.

"Stop!" I called out as Chase and Gary moved to pursuit. "You're too heavy. We need balance."

Taking a deep breath, I stepped onto the opposite platform, then onto the log itself. It began to roll beneath my feet, and I instinctively adjusted my stance, mimicking the loggers I'd seen at past county fairs.

Fawn sneered from the other end. "You think you can take me, Juli?"

"This isn't about taking anyone," I replied, trying to keep my voice steady. "It's about doing the right thing."

As we stood facing each other, a whirlwind of thoughts surged through my mind. How had it come to this? The quaint charm of New Hope seemed a world away from this surreal confrontation. While focusing on my balance, I slowly reached into my back pocket and pulled out my potential bargaining chip.

I held up the bottle of Oxy. "Is this what you're after, Fawn?"

Fawn's eyes flashed with anger. "You don't know anything!"

As Fawn's movements became more erratic to keep her balance, I pressed forward. "I know about Paul, and Eddie. And Rita."

"Paul ruined everything!" Fawn spat, her balance wavering. "He pushed me into taking steroids, didn't care I was relapsing. All for his precious gym."

My heart ached at the pain in Fawn's voice, but I needed to go further. I altered my foot position, and the log turned. "What about Eddie?"

"My supplier after I left Paul," Fawn admitted, her anger giving way to bitterness as she adjusted her posture and moved her feet. "I thought Paul would come after me, but he didn't. I made the decision to work for Eddie. Then I decided to come back to Paul, but he'd already moved on. We were supposed to run the gym together, not him and Rita!" Fawn pushed off rapidly as if running in place on the log. The log began to spin and pick up speed.

"Ivan said no," I guessed, piecing it together as my feet pedaled atop the log to keep up.

Fawn nodded, as her feet slowed down, her eyes glistening. "If I couldn't have Paul, no one would. He wasn't who he claimed to be. I was helping Rita ..."

In a desperate gambit, I tossed the pill bottle, hoping to throw Fawn off balance. But Fawn didn't flinch.

Suddenly, Major leapt into the air. I gasped, momentarily distracted. A flash of feathers caught my eye as Scallywag swooped down, snatching the bottle mid-air in his talons.

"Scallywag!" I called out instinctively, torn between focusing on Fawn and my concern for the bird's safety.

Major hit the water, the sudden splash sending a wave rippling across the water's surface. I felt the log beneath my feet lurch violently, throwing me off balance. I caught a glimpse of Fawn's wide eyes as we both teetered precariously.

"Whoa!" I cried out, my arms windmilling as I desperately tried to stay upright.

The log rolled treacherously, and I found myself dropping to my hands and knees. I clung to the rough bark, my heart thudding with an intense rhythm. I noticed Fawn had also fallen to all fours, her knuckles white as she gripped the log.

"Hold on!" Chase's voice called out from the platform.

My thoughts raced. *We're okay. We're okay. Just stay calm.* I took a deep breath, willing my racing heart to slow. The waves rocked the log, and I felt my stomach lurch with each movement.

Suddenly, a flutter of wings caught my attention. Scallywag, still clutching the pill bottle, landed gracefully on the log in front of Fawn. The bird cocked its head, almost seeming to taunt her with its prize.

Fawn's eyes widened. "Give me that!" she hissed, her voice desperate.

"Fawn, don't—" I began, but it was too late.

Fawn lunged forward, her fingers grasping for the bottle. In that instance, she lost her precarious balance and tumbled sideways into the water with a splash.

Without hesitation, I plunged in after her. The cold water shocked my system as I swam towards Fawn's flailing form.

"I've got you," I gasped, wrapping an arm around Fawn's

waist. "Stop struggling or you'll drown us both. Let's get you to the edge."

She finally calmed down enough where I could swim. As we were nearing the platform, I saw Gary reach down to help Fawn. Chase was there too, his eyes filled with concern as he extended a hand towards me.

"Are you all right?" Chase asked, his strong grip pulling me from the water.

I nodded, catching my breath. I turned to see Gary helping a shivering Fawn onto the platform. Despite everything, I felt a wave of relief. We were safe, at least for now.

———

THE SETTING SUN PAINTED NEW HOPE'S SKY IN HUES OF lavender and gold, casting a warm glow over my front porch. I sipped my wine, relishing the crisp chardonnay as it cooled my throat. Chase's presence beside me was comforting, a reminder of how far we'd come since the first day I returned home.

"I'm so glad it's over. Maybe now life can return to normal." And David could get out of town once and for all.

"Gary and Liam did a sweep around the hall of mirrors and found Fawn's duffle bag. She'd definitely been planning something. She had steroids and medical grade saline."

"What a psycho." I physically shivered. "Are you calling it pre-meditated murder?"

"She says she only wanted to make him sick so she could take care of him. Even Sam corroborated if his sugar was that high, he needed medical attention not a shot full of saline. Under normal circumstances he probably would have gotten sick. His elevated glucose was a recipe for disaster."

"What next?"

"We'll interrogate her a little more, try to get her to rat out Eddie. I can confidently say the mayor is happy now that I've released the lockdown order." Chase raised his glass and I clinked it against mine. I knew he wasn't happy about letting Eddie go free. But without a confession or proof of any drugs, it didn't matter what I saw back in Boston. But now, maybe Eddie would get what he had coming after all.

"It's funny we haven't seen Simon out walking by tonight."

"Simon? Why him?" Chase glanced up and down the quiet street.

"It seems like every time Mrs. Bailey and I are out enjoying the evening, he's always walking and stops to chat. He loves to take pictures of the sunsets."

"They are beautiful around here."

"You know," I began, twirling the stem of my glass, "Ollie's still fixated on that phantom woman from the house of mirrors. I can't help but wonder if it's just his way of coping with the stress of being a final judge."

Chase nodded, his eyes reflecting concern. "Speaking of coping, April's been calling me daily. She's convinced I'm depressed after the whole ordeal."

I couldn't help but chuckle. "Well, you don't seem depressed to me. Although, I have to admit, I've never seen Rita happier. Even David's been more attentive to her and less focused on work. It's nice to see, especially since he'll be heading to Boston soon to reopen the gallery."

My mind drifted to *The Butler's Pantry*. The café had become my anchor, a symbol of my fresh start in New Hope. "Business at the *Pantry* has been booming. Those free sample Sundays at the café are a hit."

Chase's hand found mine, giving it a gentle squeeze. "I'm proud of you, Juli. You've really made something special here."

His touch sent a familiar warmth through me, and I found myself longing for more. "This is nice, you know? Sitting here, talking. I really miss it."

I watched Chase's expression soften, affection and hesitation swirling in his eyes. "I know. I miss it too. But we both have things to figure out, more to discuss. We can't rush this."

His words hung in the air, and I felt a pang of uncertainty. I knew he was right, but it didn't make the waiting any easier.

Chase's voice pulled me from my thoughts. "I have to ask ... are there any other skeletons in Boston I should know about?"

The question caught me off guard, but I was relieved to answer truthfully. "No, Chase. No more skeletons. Boston's firmly in my rear-view mirror."

"Good," he replied, his shoulders visibly relaxing. "I'm still worried about those voodoo doll threats, though. Are you sure they've stopped?"

I waved my hand dismissively. "It was harmless, Chase. None of us have received another doll of any kind. I'm pretty sure it's over."

"You mentioned Simon earlier and I want you to know that I'm having one of Gary's connections look into him."

"Why? It's like you said before, he keeps to himself."

"Him waiting for you in the café was too coincidental for me. You know how when something doesn't sit right, you can't let it go?" He waited for me to nod, because I knew exactly what he was talking about. "Well, that's me with Simon. When his report comes back clean, I'll let this drop. But until then ..."

"Be careful what you wish for. I've learned from experience if you dig too deep, you're bound to find something you weren't expecting ... like a skeleton."

"You may be right." He smiled at the skeleton comment. "Stay alert and be careful. Don't think that just because you're in New Hope, nothing happens. It appears we're not that sleepy town anymore."

As if on cue, my phone buzzed. I glanced at the screen, a smile tugging at my lips. "It's Rita. She wants me to stop by in the morning. Apparently, she's putting the finishing touches on her stained glass rendering of *Lost Horizon*."

We drifted into a tranquil silence, the kind that speaks volumes without a single word. The last rays of sunlight painted the sky in hues of gold and crimson, casting a warm, intimate glow over us. The horizon embraced the dying light as the first stars began to twinkle. The world felt perfectly still, as if time itself had paused just for us.

"So," Chase said, breaking the quiet, "are you ready for tomorrow's pie contest? I hear the competition's fierce this year."

I grinned, eager to hear all the drama from Oliver when it was over. "Oh, I'm more than ready for life to finally get back to normal. Not to mention this is the first year both Mom and Sandy aren't in it. A new generation of winners are about to be crowned."

As we laughed and planned for tomorrow, I couldn't help but feel grateful. Despite the challenges, I was exactly where I was meant to be.

Eighteen

I snatched my jacket from the back of a chair and bolted out of *The Butler's Pantry*, the door swinging shut behind me with a soft thud. The sweet scent of cinnamon rolls from *Ringo's* mingled with the floral notes from nearby gardens, but there was no time to linger. I'd gotten so wrapped up in my latest orders, I didn't want to be late.

As I sprinted along the sidewalk that led to Rita's studio, I felt the familiar tug of worry knotting my stomach. I refused to think that the stained glass replica of *Lost Horizon* would be anything but stunning.

Reaching the studio, I skidded to a halt, the old wooden door creaking ominously as I pushed it open. "Rita?" my voice echoed softly, barely cutting through the stillness. My worry meter kicked up a few notches as the acid in my stomach churned. "Rita, I'm here!" I called, my anxiety rising.

"Hello, Juli."

I spun around to see Simon Banks leaning in the doorway. "Simon? Were you meeting Rita, too?" I relaxed slightly, thinking maybe Rita had called him to document the unveiling of the stained glass piece.

"No. I've been waiting for you."

"Me?" I forced a swallow as my mouth had gone completely dry. His lips formed an almost sinister grin which sent my worry meter into overdrive. "What's going on?" I tried to play it cool as I took a tiny step backward toward the door.

"Don't run. It will only make things worse." Simon crossed his arms; fully confident I wasn't going to bolt. Judging by the eerie feeling washing over me ... he was right.

"Make things worse?" I scanned the workshop which remained neat and tidy. Nothing seemed out of place. Except for one thing. "Where's Rita?"

"She's waiting for you in the vault. We've got everything set up." He motioned for me to move. "C'mon, no need to look so worried." This time he smiled and showed his teeth, but the ominous feeling in the air remained. When I came closer, he rested a hand on the center of my back to guide me toward the stairs that led to the vault.

"Oh, whew, so you are going to do a shoot for the unveiling?" I smiled at him as we walked, stalling, hoping to convince myself that I was imagining things. Fawn had been arrested, there was nothing else to worry about. Simon had been fine when I'd found him waiting for me at *Petite Four Paws.*

"Something like that." He pulled a chain, and the stairwell light flickered on. "Ladies first," he said with a wave of his hand.

I slowly made my way down, hating the fact he was behind me. Something was wrong, and now I couldn't turn around. I stopped halfway. "Are you sure Rita's down here? Why aren't the lights on?"

"Oh, she's down there. Everything is set up in the vault." He shoved me enough to make me quickly step down the remaining stairs.

"Hey!" I yelled when my feet hit bottom, and I caught my balance in the dim light of the basement. "What the heck, Simon."

"Time is of the essence, Juli. Let's not keep Rita waiting." He grabbed my arm and started walking. "The vault is over here."

A large steel door stood open, and only one light was on inside. I shot a curious glance at Simon, who stood there, rubbing his hands together with an almost childlike eagerness. I could only imagine the spark in his eyes if he didn't have those darn sunglasses on. He tried to nudge me forward, but this time I planted my feet.

"You need to tell me what is going on."

"I'm surprised you haven't figured it out, considering you have the sheriff at your beck and call."

"I do not."

"Well, not after today anyway." He chuckled over an inside joke only he knew the punchline for, because my worry meter had spiked to capacity.

"What are you talking about?"

"Step inside the vault, Juli. All your answers are inside." This time he shoved me so hard, I fell to my knees on the other side of the door. When I started to rise, I heard a muffled sound almost like crying. As my eyes adjusted to the low lighting, I saw Rita bound and gagged in a chair.

"Rita!" I rushed to her, and she shook her head rapidly from side to side as if in warning. My only concern was freeing her from her constraints.

"Why did you do this?" I turned on Simon, who hung back, watching the show. I worked the knot in the bandana tied tightly around her head.

"Because she's in the way. And so are you, which is why I used her phone to send you that text message last night." He paused, appearing pleased with himself. "I also sent one to David, telling him I'd be working late to finish your project. He's so enamored with Rita, he actually bought it." Simon let loose a hearty, evil, laugh.

I pulled the bandana free and faced off with Simon again, stepping forward between the man and Rita. I'd always hated the fact I couldn't see his eyes, and now I knew why. You can tell a lot about a person by their eyes. He'd been a bad man from the start.

"You'd better start explaining," I pulled my phone from my pocket, "I'm calling Chase right now."

"No, you're not. It's literally Fort Knox down here."

"I glanced at my phone. There was zero cellular signal. With a groan and a worried glance at Rita, I slipped it into my back pocket.

"What do you want, Simon."

"I came here for you, Juli. But then hearing through the small-town grapevine that Rita had an Oscar Royce, too, was an absolute bonus. I should have known it was a von Hoffster thing. Which inevitably makes my victory all the sweeter." He tapped my architectural tube.

"How did you take my painting?" Rita asked from the chair. "It's still on my wall."

"It's fake. I took advantage of you visiting David in jail and switched out the paintings. I knew you'd never catch on."

"You're never going to get away with this." I sprinted toward the doorway behind Simon. Juking in one direction then switching to the other. The exit was in sight. I was about to cross when strong arms latched around my waist and hauled me back inside.

"Nice try, Juli. You're not allowed to leave, or maybe I forgot to tell you that."

"Let me go!" I twisted and kicked my legs, arms flailing. My left hand smacked into his head, knocking his sunglasses off his face. Simon dropped me to the ground, and I gasped at the sight of him. No wonder he wore sunglasses. Without them he would have been easily identified. Simon looked vaguely familiar, but I couldn't think of where I'd seen him.

Simon had one blue eye and one brown.

"You don't know, do you?"

"No. Not yet, but I'll figure it out."

"It won't matter. You'll run out of time anyway." He swept his hand to a blinking light by the door. "See that? It's a timer. And when it runs out...BOOM. This whole place goes up with both of you in it."

"A bomb?" Rita's voice quivered.

"Why?" I glanced at the door again, only this time he stepped closer to block my way entirely.

"Let's just call you collateral damage. I have what I came here for, and I'm not leaving any witnesses or anyone snooping around my business after I'm gone."

"What about David?"

"He doesn't even know I'm here. The poor slob will be so distraught over losing both of you, he won't even think to put together the pieces." He watched me carefully as he grabbed a backpack off the floor. "I've got a little parting gift for each of you. You didn't seem to like the ones I left before, so maybe these will comfort you during your last minutes here."

"You left these voodoo dolls?" I stared in horror at the rag doll in my hand. The same hand stitching, only the faces were different. They had frowning faces and red spatters all over them.

"Hope you don't mind, but I painted those special touches myself. You see, my mother makes these dolls. They keep her busy in the nursing home. Since my brothers and I have taken over the business, the only way we could keep her out of it was to move her somewhere where she can't get out."

"Brothers?" I dug through my memory files, coming up blank.

"Evelyn," Rita said, "She's your mother."

"Evelyn Percy?" I asked and Rita nodded. "You're not Simon Percy. I met him, I would know him." But I never got a chance to meet the other brothers. "Your mother was not ready for a nursing home."

"My brothers didn't think so either, but I'm the oldest and after she took a bad fall, I convinced her to give me power of attorney. She had been meddling into our side business anyway."

"The drugs." My head began to spin. This went deeper than I ever imagined. Even Eddie was a small fish compared to the Percys.

"That's right. Eddie was easy to pay off when he wanted out. He's small potatoes compared to where we're going. And David, he's clueless and not the cutthroat businessman we thought he could be. You, Julianna, were the last piece we needed to take care of. With your connections to the police, I can't trust you to keep your pretty little mouth shut." He casually strolled to the door. "I appreciate the opportunity to steal back your art, ladies. But I must warn you, there's no way in or out once I'm gone."

"What?" I asked, fighting the fear bubbling inside me.

"He's right, Juli. The door only opens from the outside," Rita confirmed.

"Correct! Give that lady another doll!" Simon yelled. "And once I close the vault door, the timer I've placed on the outside will sync with this one in here. Should anyone try to open it from the outside, the detonator will be activated and, well, I think you're smart enough to know the rest." Simon gave us a salute and closed the vault door.

I'd never felt more defeated and scared in my entire life.

———

WITH A DEEP BREATH, I LEANED AGAINST THE COOL surface of the vault door, grounding myself. "Okay, think, Juli," I murmured to myself. I scanned the area for anything that might help us escape.

"Juli, I think we need to hurry. Help me out of this chair," Rita cried as she struggled to free her hands, but the duct tape held strong. "What's the time on that timer?"

"Thirty minutes!" Panic burst throughout my body. "Hold on!" I raced across the room to Rita, my hands trembling slightly as I fumbled trying to rip the tape. "It's not tearing. I need a knife or some scissors."

"I think there are some of my glass tools down here. Look for a small red toolbox."

"Where?" I ran from corner to corner. "Rita, where is it?"

"There!" She pointed to a metal worktable stacked with different styled frames. "On the floor!"

I tossed open the top of the toolbox and grabbed a pair of what looked like tin snips. "I hope this works." Rushing across the room, I struggled to get the large end of the snips between the sticky pieces of tape. Pressing the handle, it took four cuts to finally break the tape.

"Thank God!" Rita exclaimed when I completed the task. She leapt from the chair and rushed to the timer. "We have to find a way out."

"How? Is there another door?"

"Ugh, this house is so old. I moved things in here without really taking in the space. It was only supposed to be storage and then I used it for my more valuable items."

"That's great, but we need a way out."

"Wait, what's that line of light up there?" Rita pointed to where a wooden storage rack had been set up against a wall with stacks of totes stacked within. "Is that daylight?"

We looked at each other, giddy with newfound hope.

I wasted no time scaling the shelf. "Rita, it's a window! We need to move these totes."

Rita didn't hesitate. She climbed the shelf and together we sent totes falling to the floor. We had to clear two rows before we gained access to the window.

The very small window.

"It's so dusty and dirty I can't see outside. I'm going to try to open it." I reached up and turned the flat handle, but the window didn't budge. "It's not opening."

"Just ... maybe we can force it," Rita replied, jumping to the floor and racing back to the toolbox. She came back with a screw-driver and a wrench. "Let's try these." She handed me each tool, then climbed back up. "I can't believe this is happening. We're going to run out of time."

"No, we're not. We're two resourceful women. We're going to get out," I stated, trying to keep Rita calm. I prided myself on being good under pressure.

I had to get us out of here. We were too young to go out this way. I still had things to do with my business, my ... life. Chase's face appeared in my mind's eye, and I choked back a sob. I didn't want his last memory of me being one of disappointment and untold truths. I needed a chance to make it right.

"Juli! C'mon, I need your help!" Rita's voice and the sound of metal banging pulled me back to reality. "I got it to move a little. Let's see if we can open it now."

"Okay, let's try," I said, taking a deep breath to calm my racing thoughts. We placed our hands together on the handle of the window. "On three," I instructed, through the tension coiling in my stomach.

"One ... two ... three!" We pulled simultaneously, both of us groaning through our effort, but the window remained unyielding. The faint echoes of the outside world barely reached us through the glass. It reminded me how close we were to the festivities—yet how far from freedom we really were.

"Ugh, it's no use!" Rita jumped down, frustration etched across her face. I bit my lip, hunting for inspiration.

"Juuuuli?"

I gasped as I saw a blurry flutter of blue through the hazy dust of the window. It couldn't be. I was beginning to wonder if this crazy parrot didn't have some kind of tracker on me. And I couldn't be happier.

"Scallywag!" I tapped on the glass and then he was gone. "Nooo ..." Now it was my turn to slump. I shifted to a tote with nothing above it and sat with my face in my hands willing myself not to cry.

"Where did he go? Did he go for help?" Rita at least sounded hopeful.

"I don't know, and I can't see him."

"Break the window, Juli." Rita handed me the hammer.

I swung the hammer through the glass and it shattered, with pieces flying everywhere, then I pushed it around the entire frame to release any jagged edges. The window was big enough for a small child to get through, or maybe a crazy parrot if he ever came back. I clicked my tongue and let out a couple whistles.

"Juli's in trouble. Click-Click-Click. Troouuuble," Scallywag sang and bobbed his head from a low branch.

"Scallywag, you wonderful, beautiful bird. Go get help. Juli needs help." I pointed through the window.

"Help. Juuuuuli."

"Yes, yes, help Juli. Go get your friend Major," I said but the bird looked at me with those large eyes blinking and cocked his plumed head. "You know, Woof-Woof!" I barked.

"EEEEEKK!" the ridiculous bird screeched and flapped his massive wings.

"Juli, what is happening. The clock is ticking," Rita called from across the room.

"I know, I'm trying!"

Scallywag hopped off the branch and approached the window. I had to think of some way he could help. Then I remembered he liked shiny things. I reached around my neck and took off my silver "J" necklace, praying the bird would do the right thing.

"Look, pretty boy, what do you think?" I held it in my palm, letting the sun sparkle off the metal. "Take it to Chase." He would recognize it. The day he'd given me the key to his house, he gave me the necklace. I'd started wearing it constantly since our intermission because I refused to lose him completely.

Scallywag walked closer, occasionally stopping to prune his wings or pick at the grass.

"What is happening?" Rita groaned from below. "Do I have to come up there and kill the bird?"

"EEEEEK!" Scallywag screeched again and flapped. "Juli bad. Bad Juli."

"No, no, no. Juli good. Juli has a pretty for you." Once more I mesmerized him with the shimmer of the necklace. "I need your help, Scallywag. Please. Just take this to Chase." In one hop he surprised me and snatched the necklace from my hand. He flapped his wings and flew away.

"Juuuuuli trouble. Trouble coming!"

"Can he really do that?" Rita's skepticism hung in the air, as I climbed down from the rack. But I did notice the flicker of hope in her eyes.

"He lives up to his name no doubt. The bird broke me out of jail. I'm betting he can beat the bomb," I insisted, hoping to convince us both.

The silence felt oppressive, thickening with each passing second. Every minute we sat or paced made me realize Scallywag was a longshot. We weren't up against locked doors, there was a ticking bomb that had now reached five minutes.

"Woof-Woof-Woof!"

"Oh my gosh, Major!" I yelled and scaled the rack in record time. "Major! I'm here!"

"Scarlett!" I heard Chase's voice, and the dam of tears broke. Major appeared first, nudging my outstretched arm through the window and licking it, providing a shred of comfort. Chase knelt on the ground beside his dog, his eyes filled with determination.

"We're going to get you out. Gary's coming in," he said, his voice steady but urgent.

"No!" Both Rita and I screamed in unison. "Stop him!"

Chase's face paled with concern. "What's going on, are either of you hurt? Gary, come here!"

"There's a bomb, Chase," I managed to choke out. "Simon

tripped the vault with a bomb. We're trapped in here and if you try to open it from the outside, it will blow up."

"What? Juli, no," Chase said, his voice breaking with worry.

"Yes. We have five minutes," I said, fighting to keep my voice steady.

"That's not a lot of time, Boss," Gary said, his face drawn with fear. "We need help."

"I can do it," a strange voice cut in.

"Liam, you're still a rookie. I can't let you take that risk," Chase ordered, his tone firm.

"I can do it, sir," Liam replied, stepping forward. He was tall and lean, from what I could tell from my angle at the window, with a youthful face that belied the seriousness of his expression. His hazel eyes shone with unexpected determination.

"How do you know about disarming a bomb?" Gary questioned, his voice sounding skeptical.

"Start talking, rookie," Chase commanded, his vocal cords strained with tension.

"The short version, please!" I yelled from the vault, the seconds ticking away in my mind.

"My dad was an Explosive Ordnance Disposal Specialist in the army," Liam began, his voice steady despite the gravity of the situation. "He used to rig fake bombs when we went camping in the woods. He'd then show me how to handle and disarm them. He'd time me and if I didn't fake blow myself up, he'd let me have some beer. Sir."

The worry in Chase's voice was evident when he said, "You feel confident you can do this?"

"Yes, sir," Liam responded, his voice unwavering.

"Gentlemen, need I remind you that we're going to die anyway if he doesn't try."

Chase took a deep breath, "All right, let's do this. Liam, you have our trust. Julianna, you and Rita get as far away from the door as you can. Barricade yourselves if possible. Do you understand?"

"Yes," I confirmed as I started to climb down. Chase's hand on mine stopped me and he lowered himself onto his stomach so he could see me.

"Hey, you're going to be all right. I—"

"Me, too. See you on the other side, Lawman." I dropped to the floor. Rita and I did as we were told. I held my breath as the minutes ticked away.

What seemed like an eternity later, we heard, "Clear!"

"Is it ...?" Rita began, her breath catching with anticipation.

I bit my lip, adrenaline surging through my veins at the possibility the vault was going to open without detonating.

"What's wrong? Why aren't they coming in?" Rita asked, peering through a crack in our makeshift enclosure.

"Scarlett!" Chase yelled as he shot through the vault door. My heart raced as he pushed the totes and particle board from around us and pulled me into his arms. "Are you okay? Did he hurt you?"

"No. Rita and I are fine. But Simon—"

"Isn't Simon Banks, I know," he said, wrapping an arm around me and walking me out of the vault. I glanced over my shoulder to see Gary helping Rita as Chase continued, "I did some digging on my own. I told you something didn't set right with me. It took me several rounds of dead ends to finally get a bite on who he really was. I was going to tell you when you got back from Rita's."

"Only I didn't come back."

"No, and you weren't answering your phone, which reminds me ... I think this belongs to you." Chase held up my silver necklace, and I gathered the hair off my neck so he could put it on. "When Scallywag dropped this in front of me, I knew there was something wrong. I didn't even know you still wore it."

"I haven't until we went on our intermission," I confessed. "I must admit, I like it."

"Me too."

We stopped walking when we hit the fresh air of Rita's backyard. I wiped the rest of my tears, then glanced down at my phone. I had several missed calls from Chase and eight frantic text messages from Oliver.

"The pie contest!"

"What about it?" Chase asked. "It's got to be over by now, or close to it."

"We have to get there! Ollie tried to reach me. I have to be there to support him. I can't miss it."

Hand in hand we ran to his squad car, followed by Major and Scallywag flying high. As I sat shotgun with the sirens screaming through town, I couldn't help but smile at what a rag-tag squad of mystery solvers we were.

Nineteen

"Look!" Rita pointed, her voice barely audible over the loudness of the crowd. I followed her gaze to see Misty Shepard standing proudly behind a table adorned with colorful decorations. The sun glinted off her golden-brown pumpkin brulée pie, its smooth surface glistening invitingly.

"How does she do it?" I mused, awe lacing my voice. Misty had a knack for turning simple ingredients into culinary masterpieces, and this pie looked like the crown jewel of the contest.

"She's incredible," Rita agreed, her enthusiasm infectious. We joined the growing crowd, our hearts lighter amidst the joy that surrounded us. I felt a warmth unfurl in my chest, the tension from the vault slowly melting away.

As we edged closer, I could hear snippets of conversation—people praising Misty's skills, reminiscing about past contests, and sharing recipes. This was community at its best, where every smile and laugh stitched together the tapestry of New Hope.

"Look at her confidence," I whispered to Rita, nodding toward Misty, who was gracefully presenting her pie to the judges. "I wish I could have that kind of poise."

"Just wait until you get back to your café," Rita said, nudging me playfully. "You'll be up there one day too."

"Maybe," I replied, "I just might leave that honor in memory of my mother. I'm more content behind the scenes."

The judges gathered before Misty, their expressions a mix of skepticism and curiosity as they leaned in to take their first bites. Each subtle twist of their lips sending a flutter of anticipation through the crowd. I could almost taste the warm spices wafting from the pumpkin brulée pie, mingling with the caramelized crunch of the sugary crust.

Misty stood tall, radiating confidence with her bright smile and elegant posture. As the judges savored her creation, silence fell over the gathering. All eyes were glued to Misty's face, watching for any flicker of worry or doubt.

"Delicious!" one judge finally exclaimed, raising his head with an approving grin. "This filling is so rich and creamy!" The other judges nodded in unison, and the tension in the air shifted into something electric.

"Just a perfect balance of flavors," another judge added, and the crowd erupted in eager applause. I felt a swell of pride for Misty, who had dedicated countless hours to perfecting her craft after taking over her family's business at *The Sunflower Inn*.

"There seems to be a unanimous agreement among our judges," Ollie began, standing tall and not appearing nervous at all. "First place goes to Misty Shepard for her incredible pumpkin brulée pie!" He declared, his voice booming over the cheers and clapping.

We all joined the chorus of excitement, clapping our hands together, Chase and Gary letting out shrill whistles with their fingers. My gaze swept across the crowd, soaking in the joy of the festival, when it suddenly landed on Oliver.

He was standing near the front, eyes wide with admiration, utterly captivated by Misty. My heart skipped a beat, not entirely sure if it was the sight of Oliver or the thrill of Misty's victory that stirred something inside me. His usual easygoing charm was replaced by an intensity that made him seem more alive than ever.

Looks like someone has found his muse, I thought, a teasing smile creeping onto my lips. He stood with his hands shoved deep in his pockets, still mesmerized by Misty's triumphant moment, like he'd stumbled into a painting and couldn't quite believe it was real.

"Hey there," I said, stepping up beside him, hoping to break the spell. The warmth of the late afternoon sun wrapped around us as I gestured toward the stage. "Can you believe how well Misty did? That pie looked incredible!"

Oliver blinked, finally turning to face me, a sheepish grin spreading across his face. "It was amazing! I mean, look at that caramel glaze—perfectly done! And the way she presented it? So impressive, it's like she painted with flavors."

"Definitely!" I laughed, my heart coming alive at his enthusiasm. "I think the judges were just as enchanted. They probably had visions of autumn dancing in their heads with every bite."

"Right?" His smile widened, making his blue eyes sparkle. "Jules, she's so talented. I've never tasted anything like it. It makes me want to step up my game in the kitchen."

"Maybe you can whip up something for the next contest?" I teased, nudging him playfully.

"Ha! If only I could bake like that. My talents lie in the main course arena," he chuckled, shaking his head. Then, suddenly serious, he turned to me. "Juli, I need your advice."

"About what?" I tilted my head, curious.

"About Misty," he said, a hint of vulnerability creeping into his voice. "I can't stop thinking about her. I thought the hall of mirrors was just chance, then seeing her as a contestant was almost like fate putting us together. But now ... handing her the prize ribbon and trophy, it hit me hard. I'm kind of smitten."

"Well, she's pretty hard not to admire," I replied, trying to keep things light even as my excitement increased by his confession.

"Exactly! But how do I even approach her? I don't want to make a fool of myself," he admitted, running a hand through his sandy brown hair, a gesture I found endearing. He was definitely a catch for the right woman.

"Just be yourself," I said, my tone earnest. "You're genuine, and she'll appreciate that. Maybe start with a compliment about her pie? That's an easy icebreaker."

"That sounds simple enough," he mused, a glimmer of hope lighting up his expression. "But what if I come off as too ... forward?"

"Then just ease into it. Talk about the festival, ask her about her baking. People love sharing their passions." I smiled, feeling a warm flutter in my chest, one that came not just from my encouragement but from the way he was looking at her—a blend of gratitude and admiration.

"You always know just what to say." He paused, letting the words hang between us, and then added with a playful smirk, "Maybe I should take notes from you on how to charm someone."

"Well, I'm no expert," I snorted. "But I think you have everything you need right here." I gently poked at his heart, where his sincerity shimmered like a beacon.

"All right, I'll give it a shot." Oliver grinned, determination sparking in his eyes. "Thanks, Jules, and who knows? Maybe I'll get a date, or at least a baking lesson."

"Go get 'em!" I laughed, and for a moment, the vibrant energy of the festival enveloped us, weaving our friendship into the sweet tapestry of New Hope's summer spirit. It was a nice escape from the reality that I had almost died.

———

I STOOD BEHIND THE COUNTER OF *THE BUTLER'S Pantry*, my hands lightly dusted with flour as I arranged the last tray of freshly baked tarts and mini vegan cheesecakes, which had been a huge hit during the fair. The café buzzed with laughter and chatter, a warm cocoon of community that wrapped around me like a soft blanket. I paused for a moment, wiping my hands on my apron before taking it off to enjoy the sight of familiar faces gathered together, their smiles illuminating the cozy space.

I was still nervous because Simon was still at large, a shadow lurking in the corners of my mind. But despite the constant undercurrent of fear, I knew I had to push forward.

"Thank you all for coming tonight!" I called out, my voice rising above the din. The clinking of glasses and the rustle of paper napkins created a comforting symphony as I glanced at our guests of honor, Rita and David, who were perched on bar stools, soaking up the love from our friends.

My heart swelled. It was bittersweet to see them go.

Yes, I needed David to leave town. My fresh start, and recovery, couldn't begin if he remained in New Hope. I'd gained the closure I needed. But I hated to see Rita leave. We'd become such good friends. I understood the connection she and David still had for each other after all this time. As I gazed about the room, my eyes found Chase. As if on cue those gorgeous green eyes locked on mine, and I touched the silver "J" around my neck. The slight nod of his head and smile meant the world.

"Your support means the world to me," I continued, my gaze sweeping across the café once more. "*The Butler's Pantry* has become more than just a business; it's a place where we all come together." As the crowd quieted down, I gestured toward Oliver, who stood by the door, his shy smile encouraging. "And I'd like to thank every member of this community for welcoming my best friend and your pie contest final judge, Oliver Thompson, and allowing him to see what New Hope hospitality truly is." A few cheers erupted, and I felt a flicker of pride for how far I'd come in creating this welcoming haven. I could see the warmth in Oliver's eyes as he waved back, shy but delighted by the attention.

"With all of your support, home is starting to feel like home again," I concluded, my heart thumping with sincerity. The words lingered in the air, a promise to myself and everyone present, as I raised my glass in a toast.

"To friendship, family, new beginnings, and the magic of New Hope!"

"Cheers!" the crowd responded. As glasses clinked and laughter filled the air, I felt something shift—a sense of belonging blossoming within me, like the summer flowers blooming outside my café window.

"Juli, darlin', that was a plum perfect speech." Betty Henderson wrapped me in a giant bear hug. "It's a rightful shame about Simon Banks, or whoever he was."

"I agree, Aunt Betty," April chimed from behind her aunt, her voice as sweet as honey but carrying an edge. "Congrats on all of your success."

"Thank you, April. Sorry there was no secret admirer attached to that doll." I meant what I said, firmly believing this could be the start of a new chapter for April.

"Oh, that's all right. Chase came over and told me Simon sent the doll to me to throw anyone off track who might have made the connection. Knowing we are all friends and such, it makes sense."

"Chase came over?" I fought to keep the jealousy out of my voice, drowning any prior thoughts that April and I could ever get past our feelings for New Hope's finest. *Sorry, Mom.*

"Yes. He wanted to personally tell me. And he also informed me that Simon had lied about seeing David and Rita at *Pepper's Motel,* for the same reason." Her eyes met mine, and what came out of her mouth next made me smile despite myself. "Let the games begin, Julianna."

A mix of irritation and grudging respect flickered across my face. "Let the games begin," I echoed, meeting her gaze with a determined glint. We shared a brief, charged moment, each of us giving a small, almost imperceptible nod before she walked away to join Chase, Mayor Montgomery and Sandy Perkins.

"Hey, Juli," Gary approached with a plate of appetizers, his eyes flicking nervously to where Chase stood. "What a great party."

"Thanks Gary. And thank you for helping to save me and Rita. I really thought that was the end."

"Who knew the rookie had such skills." He shrugged and took a bite of a spring roll, trying to keep his tone light but his eyes serious.

"I'm just glad he did. I'm going to have to make him something extra special."

"He'll like that, I'm sure." Gary hesitated for a moment, his eyes searching mine. "I've got something to ask you."

"Sure, what is it?" I tucked a strand of hair behind my ear, feeling self-conscious from Gary's serious stare.

"I know you and Chase are sort of ... taking a break. I don't mean to complicate things in any way, and I mean this strictly as a friend."

"Gary, what are you trying to say?" I tilted my head, curiosity peaked.

"I still wouldn't mind cooking dinner for you sometime, if you're up to it of course. And, well, I'm here for you if you ever want to talk. About anything." His voice softened, the unspoken feelings hanging in the air.

"Gary, you're so sweet. I appreciate that, I really do. Chase and I have some things to work through. We'll just have to see where it goes. But dinner sometime sounds great." My attraction toward Gary had changed since I'd returned to town, but Chase didn't need to know that.

"Oh, and I wanted to let you know I have some of my FBI friends working on locating Eddie. Once we find him, we're hoping to get Fawn's cooperation and testimony to put him away for quite a while."

"That's wonderful!" Maybe I should have been more afraid of Eddie, but I wasn't. My eyes searched for Chase, but he was still heavy in conversation with the mayor. "I think I'm going to get some champagne," I said to Gary.

"I'll call you about dinner soon," Gary said then rushed to where Liam waved him over for another beverage, leaving me to ponder the shifting dynamics in my life and the choices I still had to make.

I poured myself a glass of champagne, the effervescence tickling my nose as I turned to survey the jubilant crowd. The laughter and chatter wrapped around me like a warm blanket, but I felt an undercurrent of bittersweetness tugging at my heart. I spotted David leaning against the railing of the patio, his untucked dress shirt flapping in the gentle evening breeze.

"Julianna," he called through the open French doors, his voice smooth and inviting. He gestured for me to join him, and with a quick glance back at Oliver, who was happily chatting with a Chase, Gary, Misty and April, I stepped outside.

"Thanks for coming out," I said, taking a moment to admire the view of the rolling hills just beyond the café. The setting sun painted the sky in hues of orange and pink, casting a warm glow over everything. It felt almost surreal, this perfect moment.

"Of course," David replied, his polished demeanor intact. "It's wonderful that you could throw a little going away party for us."

"I'm happy to do it." I took a small sip from my glass, wondering why David called me out, alone.

"I couldn't leave without properly thanking you for standing by me during that ... whole mess." His gaze was earnest, yet I caught a flicker of something else—was it guilt?

"Anyone would have done the same," I murmured, instinctively brushing a loose strand of hair behind my ear. The memory of everything we had gone through flashed through my mind. I had chosen to stand firm. Still, there was a heaviness in David's eyes that I couldn't quite place.

"Not everyone," he insisted, stepping closer, the warmth radiating from him mingling with the cool evening air. "You believed in me when I didn't deserve it, especially from you."

"That's what friends do," I replied softly, brushing off the odd feeling twisting in my gut. David wasn't normally a man of earnest conversation. He kept things light and to the point. So why was my worry meter activated?

"Still," he continued, tilting his head slightly as if weighing his words. "I want you to know how much it meant to me. You helped pull me through."

"What do you mean?" I had to ask before I took another sip.

"You stood your ground when I proposed to you."

I nearly choked as the dryness of the champagne hit the back of my throat. "Why are you bringing that up? Here of all places."

"Because it's important." He took a long sip from his own glass. "Even though you said yes, you knew you weren't ready, so you wanted it on your terms."

"I didn't realize that." I avoided David's eyes by watching the bubbles dance within my glass.

"I want you to know, I understand why you didn't keep the ring."

His statement brought my eyes to his, when I truthfully responded, "It wasn't mine to keep."

"I appreciate that. I wanted you to. I did see the future with you, Julianna. But after being here in New Hope, I see you never had that sparkle in your eyes like you do when you look at the sheriff."

"Chase?" I questioned because I wasn't quite sure what to say. In no way was I discussing my relationship status with David.

"Yes, Chase. Do you know where *I* see that sparkle?" I shook my head, and he continued, "I see it from Rita. She looks at me the way I wished you would have looked at me. Now that I've found her again, and she still looks at me that way … I don't ever want anyone else."

"David, that's wonderful, and I'm glad you've found each other again, I really am." I turned into the breeze, welcoming relief from such a personal subject.

Just then, a shadow loomed behind us, and I turned to find Chase. His eyes sharpened as he took in the scene. Concern and determination swirled in his gaze. His jaw tensed, but his posture remained steady, offering a sense of calm amidst the storm.

"David," Chase greeted, his voice steady. "Good to see you again." He offered a polite nod, but I sensed the protective energy radiating off him. "Juli, can I borrow you for a moment?"

"Sure," I replied, relief washing over me as I stepped away from David. "Please, excuse us," I said to David.

"Of course, darling, I must refill my glass and find Rita."

Chase led me toward a quieter corner of the patio. "Hey," he said, his tone lightening as we moved away from the noise. "How are you holding up after all this?"

"Better," I admitted, leaning against the stone wall, my fingers tracing the rough edges. "Tonight's a good distraction. But it still feels strange saying goodbye to David and Rita."

"Yeah, especially after everything," Chase remarked, his gaze drifting toward the horizon, where the last remnants of sunlight danced along the treetops. "To be honest, I won't be sorry to see him go." He shrugged a shoulder toward David's retreating form.

I smiled, shaking my head. "Noted."

"You did a great job tonight, by the way, the café looks amazing and everyone is raving about the food."

"Thanks. Ollie was a huge help." I felt warmth radiate in my chest. Compliments from Chase always held weight, grounding me amidst the whirlwind of emotions. "I just wanted everyone to feel at home."

"Well, you've certainly accomplished that." He paused, studying me closely, and I could sense the layers beneath his calm exterior. "But I'm worried about you. You've been through a lot since returning to New Hope."

"No more than you," I acknowledged, then reassured him, "I'll be okay," my voice steady even as my heart raced. "It's just ... there's a lot to process."

"Maybe talking about it would help," he suggested gently, his eyes searching mine, urging me to open up. There was a depth to his concern that made my chest tighten.

"Chase, I—" Something inside me faltered. Would he understand? I felt the weight of unsaid words lingering in the air like a delicate thread, ready to unravel at any moment. I leaned back, watching the twinkling white lights in the trees turn on one by one, their elegant beauty grounding me amidst the swirling emotions of the night.

Chase waited, patiently. His presence was steady, like a lighthouse guiding me through a foggy sea. I straightened up and turned to him, searching his face for reassurance.

My voice was barely above a whisper when I spoke. "I've been thinking ... about us." A flutter of nerves danced in my stomach, but I pressed on. "This intermission we've had ... it's given me time to recognize my flaw in communication. I want to do better, Chase."

He regarded me with a warmth that made my heart swell, but there was also a seriousness in his expression. "I appreciate your honesty, Juli. That means a lot." He paused, his gaze drifting briefly to the horizon before returning to mine. "But there are some important things from our history that need to be discussed."

"Like?" I prompted, knowing I could take his lead because I didn't know where to begin.

"Like how I know you well enough to understand you're not ready to dive into everything just yet." His voice was calm, measured, each word carefully chosen. "And until you are, I'm not sure what the future holds for us."

A wave of vulnerability washed over me. "I—" I hesitated, the truth resting on the tip of my tongue, but I swallowed hard instead. I didn't want to fall into old patterns, yet the fear of saying too much loomed large.

"Julianna," he said gently, his eyes locking onto mine, urging me to trust him. I felt the familiar pull of connection between us, an invisible thread woven through years of shared memories. "You don't have to rush. Take your time."

"Sometimes, I think ... I think I'm not cut out for this." The admission hung heavy between us, electrifying the air. "For being open, for letting someone in." My voice trembled slightly, betraying my struggle. "I've been so focused on keeping everything together, on making *The Butler's Pantry* succeed, that I forgot what it means to truly connect with someone. To let someone see me."

"Juli," he said gently, tilting his head slightly, as though trying to pierce through my defenses. "What are you really afraid of?"

The question struck deep. I searched his face, my heart clenching. "What if I can't be what you need? What if I let you down again?" My throat felt tight; vulnerability poured from me like a fragile stream. "I want to be here, but ... our past, *my* past, it's—"

"The past is part of who you are, of who we are," he replied, his tone unwavering. "But it doesn't define you. And it certainly doesn't scare me away." He paused, giving me a moment to absorb his words. "You're stronger than you realize, Julianna Butler. You didn't just survive; you built something beautiful here."

"But what if it all falls apart?" I whispered, my gaze dropping to the ground, where shadows danced under the twinkling lights. "What if I can't hold onto this feeling of home?"

"Home isn't about perfection," he said, his voice rich with sincerity. "It's about the people we choose to share it with. And as long as home feels like home, then I will always be here."

His words wrapped around me like my mother's embrace, igniting a flicker of hope within me. I met his gaze, searching for reassurance in the depths of his eyes. "You mean that?" I asked, my voice almost inaudible from the music and conversation filtering to the patio.

"Absolutely," he affirmed, taking a step forward, closing the distance between us. "You have nothing to worry about, Scarlett. I'm not going anywhere."

The kitchen of *The Butler's Pantry* hummed with activity, the sweet aroma of cinnamon and sugar swirling together like old friends. I stood at the counter, my hands dusted with flour as I kneaded a batch of dough. The rhythm was soothing, a comforting reminder of how far I had come in the last two months.

"Chase, could you grab the bowl of apples you chopped?" I called over my shoulder, my voice brightening at the sight of him leaning against the doorframe, arms crossed, watching me with an appreciative smile. His green eyes sparkled with mischief, making my heart skip—something that had become all too familiar.

"Of course," he replied, a playful lilt to his tone as he stepped forward. He reached for the bowl, but before he could hand it over, I felt a sudden tug at my apron strings.

"Steve!" I laughed, glancing down to see the black kitten batting at the dangling ties of my apron, his tiny white paws occasionally snagging the fabric. "What are you doing, you little rascal?"

"Looks like he wants some attention," Chase said, chuckling as

I bent to scoop Steve into my arms. I cradled him close, feeling the warmth of his fur and buzz of his purring against my cheek.

"You're such a troublemaker," I cooed, planting a kiss on his head, "but you're also so adorable." As I straightened, I caught Chase's gaze lingering on me, an unspoken question hanging between us. We were still on that delicate intermission in our relationship, both navigating the complexities that lay beneath the surface, not knowing how long it would take.

"How's the pie coming along?" Oliver's voice broke through, pulling me back to the task at hand. He stood by the stove, stirring a pot of caramel sauce with careful precision. His brow furrowed in concentration, but there was a spark of excitement in his expression.

"It's coming along nicely. Almost ready for the finishing touches," I replied, setting Steve down and quickly washing my hands at the sink. The kitten scampered away, exploring the kitchen with the carefree attitude only a young cat could possess.

"Fruit tarts are coming together nicely over here!" Misty chimed in from her station at the kitchen island, where she was arranging colorful tarts of varying shapes and sizes. Her chocolate brown hair was pulled into a messy bun, and she wore a bright apron that matched her vibrant spirit.

"Cooookie" Scallywag squawked enthusiastically and flapped his massive blue wings from inside his new cage by the sunny window in *Petite Four Paws Café*. Mrs. Bailey asked if I could bring him to the café to socialize with other people and animals. I thought it was a wonderful idea and might keep him out of trouble. A couple times a week, he came to work with me. So far, so good.

"You'll get your cookie when the baking is done," I said and offered him a sesame peep, which he dropped on the bottom of his cage.

"Bad Juuuli. Cooookie."

"Woof-Woof!" Major sat below the cage.

"EEEEKK!" Scallywag's screech was deafening.

"Just wait until the fall festival! *Savory Elegance* will be a hit," Oliver declared, over the barking and squawking, his enthusiasm infectious. He stirred the caramel again, glancing at me, his eyes gleaming with ambition. "I can already picture the menu. Now all I need is the right location."

"I'm ready for that caramel drizzle over these apples," I said. "I still have to do the lattice crust."

"What do we think about these cookies? Should we go with chocolate chip or something more adventurous?" Misty stood next to the large mixer.

"How about caramel chip cookies," Chase suggested, his voice steady and confident. "That way, you cater to both crowds."

"That's brilliant!" I exclaimed, my heart fluttering. I loved when we worked together like this, our ideas bouncing off each other. It felt easy, natural even, but I couldn't ignore the pang in my chest whenever I looked at Chase. Truth be told, I wasn't handling our intermission any better than I did the break.

"All right, then it's settled," Misty said. "Caramel chip it is!"

I turned back to my pie crust, rolling it out and cutting it into perfect strips for the lattice work while Chase joined me at the counter, our shoulders almost brushing.

"Have you heard from Rita since she sent over the stained glass piece?" Chase asked, his tone casual, but I sensed the weight behind the question. The beautiful work of art now hung prominently in my living room, a radiant reminder of everything I'd endured—and overcome.

"Yeah, she called last week," I replied, my voice softening. "She and David are doing really well bringing the gallery back to life. She mentioned how much it meant to her to create something beautiful after everything that happened. It's amazing how much life can change, isn't it?"

"*Lost Horizon*," Chase murmured, his gaze drifting to the

window where sunlight poured in. "It really does take on new meaning. Lost things are sometimes found again."

"Yes," I said, my heart swelling with hope. "It symbolizes transformation—a bridge from my past to my present."

"That's what we're all doing, right?" Oliver interjected, looking up from his pot. "Creating something new from the pieces left behind."

"Exactly," I agreed, sharing a glance with Chase that lingered just a heartbeat longer than necessary. The air between us simmered with unspoken words, yet amidst the laughter, the animals, and the clattering of dishes, I felt a sense of assurance.

Together, we continued mixing, measuring, and laughing, the bonds of friendship weaving tighter with every treat we prepared. In the heart of New Hope, amid the scents of baked goods and fresh camaraderie, I found myself standing on the threshold of new beginnings—ready to embrace whatever came next.

And *that's* another story ...

About the Author

I live in upstate New York with my very own alpha-male who puts up with my crazy author tendencies and my even crazier imagination!

I'm a firm believer in love at first sight, second chances and creating your own destiny. Isn't that what romance is all about? Being a hopeless romantic helps me write my touching, emotional and heartfelt romances. I also love a good mystery and trying to figure out whodunnit, along with the feeling of being swept into another time through historicals.

When I'm not writing, I'm in love with life on 2 wheels! I've recently gone from being a passenger to driving my own motorcycle. The thrill never gets old and I love the rush of starting that engine and taking off. Every ride is an adventure and I see the open road and world around me so differently. And of course when I'm not cruising, I enjoy a good glass of wine-or whiskey-and getting lost in a book. I also love cross-country skiing and ice-skating (although I admit to not having done either in years!) hiking, anything crafty, and competitive family game nights (scrabble of course)! And dogs. I love them and want to adopt them all!

I love to connect with my readers, fans, and other authors. Come find me and let's chat it up! Here's how: